Seven Siste
By: David Bowman
ISBN - 978-1-877546-25-9

Bluewood Publishing Ltd
Christchurch, 8441, New Zealand
www.bluewoodpublishing.com

Special Note: This book contains UK Spellings.

Also by David Bowman

Two Brothers

Carthaginian Empire Volume I

Coming soon:

Imperator

Carthaginian Empire Volume II

Carthaginian Empire Volume III

For the latest information visit:

www.BluewoodPublishing.com

Seven Sisters

by

David Bowman

To Bert
Best Wishes
David Bowman

BluewoodPublishing.com

Dedication

History is written by the winners; for if treason succeeds none dare call it treason? I find the concepts this reveals to be fascinating. I can bore the teeth off anyone at twenty paces at parties if you get me going. Hopefully, I won't bore you here. My thanks to the team at Bluewood Publishing for giving me the opportunity to put my theories into practice. My thanks as ever to the people who encouraged me to write as a means of escaping the sometimes dreadful realities of life. I truly hope you enjoy reading this story as much as I did writing it.

Prologue

Crastus knew he could wait no longer. He adjusted the close fitting silver breastplate that marked him as a Commander of the Empire. Nodding to his aides, he walked through the colonnade to where his coal black stallion stood, angrily whickering at the groom that held his reins.

As he swung his forty-three year old, campaign-worn body into the saddle, the panorama of the city spread out before him. The late autumn Mediterranean sun glistened and gleamed on the city's stonework terraces where they sloped down to the river Pescara below. Beyond the city walls, he could, from his vantage point, see the fortresses that guarded the approaches to what had been the summer capital of the empire for the last three hundred years. The whole complex known throughout the empire as the 'Seven Sisters' was by far the strongest defensive position outside of Rome itself. If he stayed, he knew the remnants of the Fifth and Seventh legions could hold it for a considerable time; but the might of the Pretender's army was bearing down on him along the coast road barely four miles away.

To preserve this 'jewel of the empire', he must give it up, and on orders from the Emperor. Valerian had yesterday issued the proclamation that declared the city of Zampetta an open city. Now, they all hoped the scars of civil war which was tearing the empire apart would at least bypass this beautiful place, and by falling back allow his outnumbered troops to join the Emperor's and swing the tide back in their favour.

His aides fell in behind him as he nudged the stallion into motion. They clattered through the open and deserted forum and began the winding, gentle descent to the south gate. As they exited the gate, the remainder of the first cohort of his own Fighting Fifth legion fell in and they picked up speed. The causeways linking the city to its forts were deliberately narrow and doglegged, standing at least five feet clear of the fertile soil contained behind the curtain wall. They clattered at a steady canter past the inner gate of the middle fort, AnnMarie, and following the deliberately crooked road, wound their way to the outer gate next to it. They cantered on through and began the slow and gentle climb up the grassy south side of the river valley. The fortresses stood with their inward-facing gates open forlornly behind them. The city gates were also open a steady stream of refugees trickled out, leaving by the river road, scared that the oncoming legions would ignore the protective provisions of the proclamation.

Crastus reined in as he reached the crest of the hillside and looked back, vowing silently to return. Motioning to his bodyguard, they followed his battered legions south and away.

Chapter 1 - Rome

He paused in the colonnaded shade at the top of the steps before entering and methodically checked over each detail of his uniform. If one fastening or buckle was out of place, he was sure that Valerian or one of his cronies would notice and decide that this was a deliberate insult. Satisfied with his appearance, he nodded courteously to the Centurion commanding the Praetorian Guard detachment manning the doors, as the man marked his name off of the list.

The nubile slave in the golden tunic glided ahead of him. Crastus could not decide which display impressed the most, the mosaics on the floors or this creature's statuesque legs. The gossamer tunic barely reached mid-thigh and hinted at delights concealed within, but like all palace slaves, she was beyond reach. To touch would bring disfavour or even death. These guides were pampered slaves, true, but slaves nonetheless. Untouchable now, but Crastus had heard stories of what happened to these women when their looks faded or they otherwise displeased the emperor. Handed over to the inner circle of cronies, their fate was unenviable. He shuddered and followed, knowing he was unlikely to have the emperor's favour. Not after such a large portion of the Pretender's army had escaped the recent battle at Salerno.

He was shown to the entrance of the throne room, and the beautiful apparition bowed and left him. He had not needed such a guide, having been here many times before, but to wander unescorted through the palace would have been unthinkable. He pretended not to notice the pair of ubiquitous Praetorian Guards that had followed him at some ten paces or so all the way from the palace entrance.

The throne room was impressive, opulent even, but Crastus had always considered the jewel-encrusted golden throne of the Emperor vulgar and definitely not in good taste. He didn't let a flicker of such thoughts cross his face as he waited with the others summoned to audience for his turn. He did not have long to wait. Gaius was in control of Valerian's schedule and, as such, had orchestrated Crastus's arrival to perfection.

The current audience victim in front of the emperor stuttered in an attempt to explain to an increasingly irritated Emperor why the southern grape harvest was falling short in both quantity and quality this year. Eventually, the Emperor had had enough. For a small man, his voice was powerful and anger made him especially loud.

"Enough!" The shout echoed off the walls of the lavish throne room. "Send me a report, and don't pad it with your feeble blathering, man. Just tell me what you intend to do about it, and before you ask, the budget is too tight to throw more money at any esoteric solution - just do it!"

Even the shaken southern citizen unused to court etiquette knew a dismissal when he heard it. Giving the required three genuflections, he backed fifteen paces away before standing upright, turning and with as much dignity as he had left, walked out.

Aggravating the emperor was not a recommended activity for any functionary, but being told to solve the problem or else, was not a good sign. As soon as he reached the doorway, he sped up and the poor soul almost ran from the palace.

On the throne, Valerian sipped from the golden goblet of watered wine and glowered at the back of the retreating man. He looked round the room and Crastus felt the Emperor's eyes fasten on to him, noting his arrival, and no doubt noting the timing of that arrival, too.

"Crastus Titus Galba, Commander of the Empire's Fifth Legion. Victor of Foggia, Ravenna and Salerno," called the Chamberlain in the voice reserved for the occasion. He gave his cousin Crastus a wink as Crastus took his place at the salutation line inlaid in ebony in the marble floor.

"You may approach." The emperor did not sound vexed anymore, Crastus noted as he began the ritual abasement followed by five steps and repeat that brought him into the close proximity of his ruler. As ever then the consummate acting skills of Valerian had been used to the full and perhaps the scurrying dignitary had less to worry about than he thought. Then again, perhaps not.

"Five years have passed since we reluctantly ordered you to abandon the Seven Sisters after your unfortunate defeat at Ancona," intoned Valerian.

Crastus stared impassively back. True, the Pretender's army had roundly defeated him at Ancona, but his victory at Ravenna the following spring had turned the tide. His recent decisive victory at Salerno had subsequently won the war for this man in front of him. The man who ruled the known world and whose influence spread far beyond it.

"With the Pretender dead by his own hand at Salerno, it is time we regained what we were forced into giving up." Valerian was obviously speaking for posterity here. Out of the corner of his eye, Crastus could see the team of Imperial scribes copying down every word. "We intend to celebrate the Summer Solstice in the palace in Zampetta. You will facilitate this as a means of atoning for the earlier loss. Do you understand the commission you are being granted"

The rumoured operation was now out in the open. Crastus had been handed the poisoned chalice and the gasps and buzz of whispered comments the announcement caused were clearly audible. The chamberlain slammed the end of his staff of office down onto with a crash and silence ensued.

Crastus watched the Emperor's expression with blank faced concentration Frustration at the hesitation edged onto the Imperial face. As his arm rose and his clenched fist crashed into his chest in military salute, he uttered the only response possible in the position he was in.

"At your command, sire!" His own parade ground trained voice boomed through the room. "The Fifth and its engineers will march within forty-eight hours."

Quartered in the barracks on the Viminalis hill, his legion was already prepared. He felt sure that Valerian was well aware of this but chose not to reveal his hand completely.

The thin lipped smile from Valerian awaited the question they both knew would be asked. Both men knew one legion was not going to be enough. Intelligence and Crastus's own observations on the field of Salerno showed the bulk of three legions had escaped the slaughter at the end of the battle. Although only two were supposed to be at Zampetta, the location of the third, the Eleventh, was not yet certain and that was a worry.

Crastus didn't hesitate.

"Sire, I will need more than a single legion to dispossess the remnants of the Pretender's army at the complex in Zampetta."

He paused, as much for the sake of the scribes as to let this sink in. Murmurs rose again and were just as quickly silenced by the crash of the butt plate of the staff hitting the floor.

"May I take it that the Seventh, Twenty-forth and Twenty-Fifth legions are detailed to the campaign as well?"

Valerian and his advisors had obviously considered this question carefully as well. It was impossible that they would denude the defences of Rome to provide Crastus with sufficient force, especially if they became loyal to Crastus first and the Emperor second. Having won one civil war by the skin of his teeth, the Emperor would never risk another with the commander who had won it for him. He had to provide Crastus with sufficient force to have a chance of winning the campaign without providing him with a platform to launch a campaign for the throne itself. Crastus knew he had to ask for more than he would get.

"The Seventh is detailed to your command and can march with you. Claudius will lead it as second-in-command to you. Schonberg and his Seventeenth are on route from the mountains around Perugia and will meet up with you at L'Aquila. That will provide sufficient force for a competent general to defeat the remnants of an already beaten army."

Crastus nodded in acceptance. He would have preferred four legions for the mission, butthe three legions named would be enough provided he could keep the casualties down. The Twenty-forth and Twenty-fifth were garrison troops – good enough in defence but not first rate in attack. Claudius's Seventh and Schonberg's famed Seventeenth were a much better class of legion; almost as good as his own. Within the confines of Italy, it certainly looked like he would command an army comprising the best three legions available. The Second and Forth were of equal calibre but were both stationed too far away. The Second was on duty on the Rhine frontier and the Forth was in Palestine. Neither could be brought back in time.

"The remnants of the Pretenders army have retreated to the Pescara valley, so you should have no trouble getting your forces there and discharging your commission on time."

The sly grin was back on his face as Valerian intoned Crastus' fate. Valerian had put the situation out in the open for the whole court to see. If Crastus won again, he would be back in favour until the next time the Empire needed its premier fire-fighter. If he didn't, his life, his family and his lands could be forfeit.

Crastus saluted one more time. "By your leave, sire!"

He backed away the required fifteen paces, genuflecting every five paces as protocol dictated. As he turned, the chamberlain's assistant handed him his golden baton of office, which would be fastened onto the front of his breastplate, and his commission. Once the baton was attached to his armour, his power would be second only to the Emperor's as long as he stayed within the bounds of his commission.

He would not be required to salute or return salutes of any officer in the entire empire save for any others similarly accoutred.

Then, he was outside the door where another golden nymph waited to lead him out into the real world again. The ubiquitous guards followed and at the door, a sergeant-at-arms returned his sword to him with a flourish. It would have been unthinkable to enter the throne room bearing weapons even if he was the premier general of the empire and Valerian's staunchest supporter.

Chapter 2 - Staff

Following his audience, with the Emperor, Crastus lost no time on the walk from the palace to the Viminalis barracks where his own Fifth legion was currently quartered. The old Rubicon rule had been suspended over the last hundred and fifty years of internal strife, and there were now always at least four legions stationed in and around Rome.

As he approached the gate, he gestured at the guards who were already moving to open it for him. As he passed, the 'centurion of the day', who today happened to be his old friend Maximus, he murmured, "Staff call in five minutes."

Continuing across the enclosed parade ground to the colonnaded conference area at the right hand corner, he entered and took his place at the head of the long table and laid his golden baton and commission in front of him.

Outside, Maximus sprang into action, issuing rapid fire orders in a voice that could be heard across the whole barracks, sending over a dozen orderlies scrambling to locate the other senior officers of the legion.

Crastus spent a few minutes relaxing and gathering his thoughts. He had known that Valerian could not leave the remnants of the rebel forces untouched. The Seven Sisters complex at Zampetta was the strongest fortress in the whole of Italy, save for Rome itself. The advances in military engineering over the last few years rendered those fortifications more susceptible to attack, though no one was certain just how far. There had to have been substance behind the rumours of the Emperor's intentions. There had never really been another candidate for the job; Claudius could have been chosen but was too far out of favour, and the other legion commanders in the region were less experienced. Crastus knew that failure would belong to him and him alone.

The staff began to file in. His Tribunes, led by Leander took their accustomed seats down the left and the senior centurions, led by Maximus, the *primus pilus* himself down the right. There were gaps. Crastus raised his eyebrow.

The *primus pilus* caught the signal before the younger men could react.

"Carus is in the city chasing a flour supply contract, Julius is on leave as his son was born in the early hours and Septimius is in the infirmary with a gash to his arm following an encounter with yet another overzealous recruit in sword practice."

The staff collectively chuckled at their absent comrade's not uncommon misfortune. He took such pride in his own prowess with the sword and it was not that unusual for him to suffer on the training ground in some way. But by God, he could train men!

"What name has Julius given to his son?"

"Agrippa"

Crastus nodded and raised a glass of watered wine in toast to the newborn

"Here's to Agrippa, another young son of Rome, destined to die on a foreign field in the service of the empire."

The men present in the room scrambled to their feet and raised their own goblets in tribute.

"Hail Agrippa, *Ave Romani*!"

Crastus then began the briefing they had been anticipating for days.

"We, along with the Seventh under Claudius, will march in forty-eight hours to recapture Zampetta. Schonberg and his Seventeenth will join us on route."

He paused to let the critical facts seep in, they had been contingency planning the campaign for days based on either three or four legions. Some of the planning was now obsolete; they were going to attack with only three legions. There were sighs of relief that Valerian had at least not saddled them with one or more of the poorer quality garrison units.

"From today, we have exactly one hundred and thirteen days to achieve this as Valerian intends to celebrate the Summer Solstice there."

The unspoken threat wasn't missed.

"The main plan will remain as discussed. We need to envelop the Seven Sisters as soon as we arrive. I had hoped to have a fourth legion in reserve, but we will have to manage with the three we have. Valerian has given us Claudius' Seventh which together with the Fifth will envelop the Sisters from the south whilst Schonberg's Seventeenth will hold the north bank. Current intelligence has not changed; there are the remains of two legions, the Twelfth and Fourteenth, holding the Sisters and the City. The mostly intact Eleventh is somewhere to the north of the city, but we don't know exactly where and that is a worry. However, Schonberg should be able to screen us and prevent a surprise attack. I have separately arranged for Actas's auxiliaries to screen him which should provide a sufficient trip wire defence for all of us.

"We move out in two days. We will collect the bulk of the horses as expected from the Esquiline remounts as we exit Rome by that gate. Maximus, get the horse handlers out there to cull sufficient mounts and remounts for the entire legion. I'm sure that Claudius will be doing the same. I don't expect to find them better mounted than us."

Grins now went down the table. The inter-legion rivalry for the best horses was something they were all familiar with and they certainly did not want to lose out to their main rival.

"Nothing stays behind. That includes the Sky Nest and all the running gear for the catapults. I'm sorry, Cesca, your lads will have a hard time in the mountains, but that can't be helped."

Cesca and Maximus shrugged. They weren't in the least surprised.

"Do we have enough bullocks for the carts?"

Cesca nodded this time, as always the engineering cohort were ready. Unlike the front line cohorts, Cesca's men needed to keep their mounts and draft animals near to the equipment and they were penned immediately to the north of the barracks.

"Right, any questions?"

"Order of march?" Trust Maximus to be ready to ask before any other could frame their questions.

Before he could answer, Crastus spotted his second-in-command hurrying through the gate and across the parade ground. Catching Leander's eye, he nodded to the door and the younger man quickly left to bring Carus up to date before he joined the discussion.

"The third cohort will lead and join the tenth at the remount depot to help prepare the horses for departure. The others will follow in standard march sequence."

"Daily progress?"

"I intend to stop at the first camp on the Cispius way so as to shake out any issues and after that every camp. I know that we can move at least twice as fast, but I want the siege and baggage trains to keep up and fifteen miles a day through the mountains is a hard slog for them as it is. It is pointless for a purely cavalry formation to invest the fortress complex. We can do nothing without the siege train, so we may as well travel with it.

"We may be in a hard fight as soon as we get there and I want the men rested and ready. I expect the campaign will be fought on foot at the walls of the forts, but I want the horses well rested too just in case."

The likelihood of the remnants of the Protectors army, or even just the currently missing Eleventh, coming out to meet him on open ground, was low. Crastus was indisputably the living master of cavalry tactics within the Empire and no one in their right mind would attack him with inferior numbers.

Leander retook his seat and Carus joined them, too.

"As we all know there are three or four good ambush points in the final approach to Zampetta, what are our plans there?" Carus asked as soon as he had taken his seat.

"Actas will be joining us at L'Aquila with Schonberg. His scouts will flush out any would-be ambushers and, if they are massed in force larger than he can handle, we will move up and destroy them. After all, every one of them we can eliminate outside of the complex is one less to defend it!"

Wolfish grins met this comment. In this mood, nobody would want to face the Fighting Fifth, who relished the opportunity to live up to their nickname. Crastus saw his officers were as ready as they could be and in the right frame of mind for the coming campaign.

The meeting dissolved into a flurry of detailed discussions covering the myriad of details facing an army about to march.

Crastus sat back and watched his highly efficient staff deal with the minutiae and began planning how he would deal with the political machinations and repercussions of the campaign. Claudius and Schonberg, the commanders of the other legions detailed under his overall command, were experienced generals in their own right. Not being of patrician descent, Schonberg would go no higher than his current post and, rather than resent this, seemed to revel in the freedom it gave him. Claudius would like this command himself, but was fully aware of the political implications for his future. Crastus would take the fall if the campaign failed, but Claudius would want a share of the glory that would accompany victory.

Chapter 3 - Journey

Over the rest of that day and the whole of the next, the barracks on the Viminalis hill was a hive of activity. Claudius and the Eighth were quartered in the more outlying barracks on the Caelian hill and the level of activity there matched that of the Fifth. Claudius and Crastus conferred on a regular basis, meeting twice a day

Claudius was very much an extrovert, right down to the seventeen hand, black stallion he rode for ceremonial duties, as well as the elaborate breastplate that marked out his patrician status. Provided he could shine on this campaign and probably the next, he would certainly hold the command baton before much longer. A couple of years younger than Crastus, he spent a considerable portion of his time on his own appearance, unlike the weather-beaten cragginess of the latter. Currently in disfavour for a dalliance with a prominent senator's wife whose pregnancy was well advanced. An old war wound prevented such happenstance in the senator's case, the chance to escape the city was something to be relished by the most likely candidate for the fatherhood.

Crastus, known for simplicity, his most audacious victories on the battlefield were masterstrokes of straightforward brilliance; while Claudius, on the other hand, was the master of deceptive planning. He would often use multi-level feints within feints to draw the enemy in the wrong direction before the killing stroke was delivered. Both acknowledged the competence of the other, and the validity of each approach depending on circumstances.

The following morning, the first day of the march was unusually overcast for the time of year. The looming clouds, although high in the sky, seemed ready to weep rain at any moment. Thankfully, the rain held off as the long columns of men and wagons formed up.

An entire legion on the march was an impressive sight. With most of the horses kept outside the city for practical reasons, the men marched on foot carrying the bulk of their equipment. At the front of each century marched the standard bearer. Clad in the traditional animal skin which would be shed when mounted, he was always the most physically impressive man in the unit. Behind the century came three carts carrying the saddles and riding tackle of the unit. Once the men were mounted, these carts would carry the men's personal kits and additional stores. Every tenth century was lead by the cohort's standard which was more ornate still. The third and ninth cohorts had gone on ahead the previous day to assemble the necessary mounts. Bringing up the rear were the bullock carts of the Tenth which carried the heavy cordage and metal components of the catapults, ballistae and the rest of the siege train. These would be assembled using local timber on site. The only exception to this was the Sky Nest observation platform which needed seasoned timber. As a result, its complete component parts were shipped in three wagons and its crew was commanded by the first centurion of the cohort, in this case, Cesca.

In total, the column stretched for nearly seven miles as it threaded its way through the broad streets of the city towards the Cispius gate. Indeed, the leading elements were well clear of the gate and heading for the assembled horse handlers and their charges before the engineering unit had formed up. The gate itself was an impressive sight. Originally built as part of the old Aurelian wall, it had been augmented by two massive fortresses on either side of the road. With the advent of gunpowder, these fortresses were not as impregnable as they had been, and now there were swarms of slaves all over them as the garrison engineers worked tirelessly to strengthen them with earthworks.

Claudius's Seventh left the city by the more southern Oppius gate and wound its way towards the vast open area that comprised the remount depot from the south. Dealing with nearly twenty thousand men trying to saddle and mount an equal number of horses dictated a certain amount of disorder, but this was a standard procedure for the legions.

Crastus lead the first mounted units of his legion east towards the waiting mountains and their fate. Behind them, organised chaos continued as each successive cohort shook itself out into marching order and followed suit. Claudius's Seventh kept pace with Crastus following a road that diverged for a few miles before rejoining at the chosen evening camp site.

The first day's march of only ten miles was designed to allow the force to deal with any last minute hold up and to shake down into marching rather than barrack discipline. There were always a few issues to sort out and it was not uncommon to spot the odd black eye or facial bruise among the troops over the next couple of days as order was enforced by the centurions. The officers turned a blind eye to such things.

Over the centuries, the legions had established regular camp sites spaced every fifteen miles or so on all the roads around Rome. The distance varied only by local terrain. The ditch, earthwork and stone wall fortifications were large enough to hold two full legions and their mounts. Within the camp, the layout was always the same and the lead cohort of each legion knew its duties. The first order of the day was to dig the latrine trenches and police the site ready for the arrival of the rest of the legion. Each cohort would lead the march in turn; after all, nobody actually enjoyed the job, nor that of filling them in after the rest had left the following morning!

Although the siege train marched with the legion, the baggage train carrying the spare arrows, projectiles and the rest of the supplies would follow a day behind. All of the men carried enough rations for seven days in the packs they carried behind them on the saddle and would replenish these rations from the storehouses kept at L'Aquila. Once the Pretender had been pushed out of the mountains, one of the first items on the order of business had been to re-establish the military supply depots there. Forage would normally be a worry for this many horses, but the spring grass was long and green and not a problem provided the legions kept on the move. When they arrived and established siege lines, it would be a different matter, one that Crastus was safe turning over to Carus. The logistics expert would normally take little part in any fighting, usually to his own displeasure, unless Crastus was in some way incapacitated. His role was behind the fighting troops but was nevertheless vital.

One small change to the original plans had been made, however. Schonberg was no longer meeting them at L'Aquila. Instead, he followed a more northerly route from the mountains which would put him onto the fertile plain to the north of Zampetta on the same day that Crastus and Claudius arrived from the south-east. Although this deprived Crastus of Actas's scouts who would be swinging to the north of Schonberg, he was confident that his own scouts would be more than sufficient.

Each day, the legions marched from one camp to the next, sometimes marching in glorious sunshine, sometimes in drizzle. Eight days later, they arrived at the final camp site seven miles short of Zampetta and here, this close to the enemy, the guard was doubled.

Tomorrow, they would arrive before the walls of Zampetta itself and the siege would begin.

Chapter 4 - Arrival

They set off from the camp just after breakfast and just over two hours later, the command party crested the final small hill. A vast panorama laid itself out before them. In the foreground, the skirmishers of the Fighting Fifth spread out on the gentle rolling green hillsides that sloped down to the middle distance where the grey stone walls of the nearest fort rose from the long grass.

Behind those walls, in his mind's eye he could see the anthill like convulsions as the defenders reacted to his army's presence. Beyond this fort, he could see the city rising in terraces from the river Pescara itself. Wavering in the heat haze, he could make out the twin river forts, Gabrielle and Beatrice, where the giant sluice gates were being hurriedly closed to flood the land between the forts. A quick scan showed few surprises as the fortresses looked mainly unchanged in the five years since the loyalist legions had been forced to retreat from the area.

Sighing sadly, Crastus turned in his saddle and motioned to one of the waiting staff.

"Send the Tenth here. I want the Sky Nest erected now, and the headquarters will be set up on the reverse slope."

As the officer galloped off, he returned to his study of the formidable defences laid before him. Before long, the creaking of the ungreased suspension of several heavy wagons and the solid tramp of two hundred or so men could be heard approaching from the rear. The headquarters wagon veered off slightly to the right a couple of hundred yards below the crest of the hill. The much heavier wagons carrying the observation platform, pulled by ten oxen, forged their way to the crest. His bodyguards parted to allow the huge rumbling carts and entourage access to the top of the hill.

The centurion in charge approached Crastus as he sat on his horse watching the drill with a slight smile. The centurion banged his fist to his chest in salute and waited for the next order. Crastus knew what he wanted.

"I think seven sections will be fine, Cesca, thank you."

The Centurion saluted, turned and bellowed out the order. Grins wreathed the faces of his team who were quite happy that they were only going half as high as they could.

Crastus dismounted and turning his back on the busy men moved to the front edge at the crest of the hill and resumed his survey of the terrain in front of him. A small hand gesture brought his senior staff forwards on foot to join him.

"Right, gentlemen, there is our target. We have one hundred and two days left to take it. I know we already developed a plan, but study what is in front of you. Are there any changes in the fortifications and layout before us? We need to know if they materially alter our plans. Full staff meeting will be at dusk."

Crastus now turned away and left his staff studying the layout in front of them. Half of them had been with him five years ago when they had retreated from this very spot. Most of the others were seeing the impressive layout for the very first time.

He watched as the practiced routine of erecting the observation platform was proceeding with great haste. Already the carts had been unloaded and the central cart, the base for the platform had been levelled and fastened down.

The sections of the uprights had been laid out and were being pegged together and attached to the cart. Shortly after the massive cross member was attached to these uprights and with the ropes fastened, the whole rig was hauled into its vertical position.

Within minutes, the basket was attached and the observers waited for their orders.

Cesca grinned and saluted; he knew his team had set a near-record time. Crastus returned the grin as he acknowledged the salute and said in his best parade ground voice.

"Bit slow today, Cesca?"

Knowing their commander's dry wit, the panting men took it for the compliment it was, knowing that a cask or two of ale would now be theirs for the evening.

Despite his forty-seven years, the one-handed leap that carried him onto the bed of the cart could not be matched by Leander, the much younger officer following him. After they climbed into the basket, the winches whirled into action and the four men were borne smoothly aloft.

The extra seventy feet of height above the ground gave Crastus and Leander a much better view of the complex. The small hilltop was only just higher than the tallest towers of the nearer fortresses. Now, the extra height enabled them to see into parts of the forts and the activity beyond and around them.

"Tell me what you see." ordered Crastus. The less experienced officer would need longer to confirm their expectations. This way, Crastus helped train the next generation of commanders.

"On the far left, I can see Claudius's Storming Seventh taking up positions in good order from the river's edge two leagues closer to us. Facing them, Dominique looks relatively unchanged since five years ago, although the gate looks to have been reinforced again. The curtain wall between Dominique and Isabelle looks rather worn in places and ought to fall easily to a swift attack."

"Perhaps," interjected Crastus, "but to what end? Controlling the curtain wall gains us nothing. Go on."

"Isabelle itself looks like there is new stonework along the top of wall and I think its walls are higher. I can't tell from here if they are thicker. The curtain wall connecting to AnnMarie in front of us looks in very good nick."

"AnnMarie was always the most formidable of the fortresses, and it looks certain from here that its walls have been added to by as much as five feet. The Fifth are drawn up in front of us are extending out to the river facing Gabrielle. Gabrielle and Beatrice are both hives of activity as they are raising the gates to dam the river. The land between the forts and the city will flood within hours and will be four or five feet deep behind the curtain wall within thirty-six hours. I can see the dust on the other side of the river as Schonberg's Seventeenth legion manoeuvres into position facing Claudine, Eliane and Beatrice. The rest of the curtain walls and causeways look well maintained and the city walls themselves are in good order."

He paused and looked to Crastus for confirmation he had covered all of the salient points.

"Are you sure Schonberg can hold that length of front? You have given him twice as much ground to cover on that side of the river as the two legions combined on this side."

A wry smile touched Crastus' face.

"I don't want Schonberg's men to invest them too tightly. With Galerius the Pretender dead by his own hand, I would rather the Twelfth and Fourteenth legions took the chance and flee to the north rather than stay and fight because they have no other choice. The forts on that bank have never been successfully stormed from outside. We must win here on this bank. Schonberg's men screen the far bank and hopefully prevent the missing Eleventh legion from arriving and reinforcing them. Actas's auxiliaries are screening still further out. If Valerian had not rescinded the Aurelius doctrine last month, we could have walked in unopposed."

Crastus allowed Leander time to take in the panorama laid out before them as the basket swayed in the gentle breeze.

"Now, Leander, tell me what more you see, and why I was so insistent on bringing this heavy equipment through the Doga Pass in spring."

Leander took a deep breath; this was almost like a graduation test on the way to his own legion command.

"You can certainly see more that I thought from here," he remarked, stalling for time whilst he arranged his thoughts.

"I think they are massing cavalry behind the postern gate at Dominique. Are they going to sally?"

"Good spot – signaller send a message to Claudius, Cavalry massing at Dominique." One of the signallers began to semaphore the attention to orders signal and as soon as it was acknowledged began sending the message. Crastus and

Leander returned their attention to in front of them as the Seventh began to adjust their lines to match the potential threat.

"Sir? I can't see the western boom across the river." Leander suddenly realized a chink in the defences. Crastus nodded and ignored his aide's obvious excitement.

"Yes, our spies reported that they had a serious problem over the winter with the winding mechanism. It's seized solid. They cannot deploy the boom. It doesn't matter as the archers on the river walls of Dominique and Claudine can effectively prevent a river assault in daylight and torches will provide enough light at night for the same slaughter. Look closely at AnnMarie."

Leander peered at AnnMarie through his telescope, desperate to see whatever it was that his commander had already spotted. Then it struck him. With rising excitement, he blurted out.

"The extra height on the walls – The fools! They've not buttressed! It's almost like an eggshell; we could crack and peel them out of that position."

Crastus smiled inwardly at his enthusiasm but let no emotion show as he waited for his subordinate to see the rest of the trap he had spotted with his first glance at AnnMarie.

When Leander was not forthcoming, Crastus prompted him gently. "Look at the buildings behind the walls.

A look of comprehension dawned. "They've been extended out to the wall. Any breach would become a killing pocket. Once through the wall, they could not fan out. The press of men coming in would prevent information coming out and it would be a slaughter!"

"Even so, AnnMarie is a weak point, Leander. They may have set the walls up as death traps, but when you look closely at the east tower where it joins the curtain wall, what can you see?"

Leander, like most of his predecessors, sweated as the questions fired at him without pause began to sap at his confidence. Try as he might, he could not see what Crastus was driving at.

With a sigh, Crastus pointed out what he found blindingly obvious. Still, he thought, at least here a mistake caused Leander anxiety. In his later career, it could very easily lead to defeat, disgrace, even death for him and possibly for a whole legion. It was time to put him out of his misery.

"Look very closely at the way they dovetailed the stonework of the curtain wall into the tower corner when the fortress was constructed. The constant flooding and draining of the land behind the curtain wall has caused a certain amount of subsidence and the joints have pulled apart a little."

Leander finally saw what his commander was getting at.

"Yes, I see now! A small group of men could ascend that as if it was a staircase, I think some of the cracks extend up the side of the tower above the curtain wall too. A surprise attack might carry the tower in its entirety. Of course, yes, if the attack was at night and silent, it would be relatively easy."

"That's right, that wall has been like that for years. The Pretender's army has never had the time to put the walls into better repair, so that weak point is the reason we will attack AnnMarie first as planned.

Crastus signalled for the basket to be lowered as, off in the distance, inside the river fort he could see the cavalry dismounting having realized they had been spotted.

Chapter 5 - Ditch

As the light faded, the sound of fast approaching hooves could be heard outside the headquarters tent. Crastus stretched to ease the muscles that had knotted during the several hours he and Leander had spent bent over the map table. The horses stopped about twenty yards short of the tents. The challenge and counter pierced the still twilight. The more guttural tones of the Latin in the response told Crastus that Schonberg was reporting in from the other side of the river having used the ford a couple of miles upriver.

Indeed, it was the big blonde legion commander of near pure northern Germanic stock who brushed aside the entrance curtain. Stepping into the lamplight, he drew himself upright and saluted. Not waiting for a response, he stepped further into the tent, a huge grin splitting his face.

"Well met, Crastus," boomed the commander of the Seventeenth.

Crastus rose from the writing table under the brightest lamp in the tent.

"Well met indeed, Schonberg," replied Crastus, answering the grin with one of his own. "How fares the North bank?"

"Well indeed. We have then invested, and the men have made a good start on the earthworks. At the western end, the earthworks and ditch are complete for nearly a mile. In their shoes, I would have sallied from Claudine to interfere with us, but they've been quiet all day."

"Good. And further east?"

"My pickets cover the whole front back to the little escarpment and my surveyors have chosen the line for the rest of the works which we should be able to complete in the morning."

"Has Actas made contact?" enquired Crastus.

"Yes. His patrols are ranging as far as seven miles further north and right to the coast without any contact with the Eleventh. Are you sure they will try to come back here?"

"Wouldn't you if it was only fortified place your side still held?"

"No, it would be like joining the rats in the cage," laughed the big blonde man. "They know they're doomed in the city, and doomed if they meet us on open ground. I expect they'll quietly disband and we'll see a few recruits with familiar faces showing up soon enough."

Leander quietly filled two silver goblets with watered wine. Waiting until the natural pause in the conversation, he slipped into the well lit area and handed them out. Crastus sipped his gratefully but, as always, his companion noisily gulped his down and handed the empty goblet back. Schonberg knew his manners, or lack thereof, shocked most of the patrician born senior officers he served with but didn't care. Even after several Spanish born emperors more than six hundred years ago the likelihood of him rising to anything higher than command of a legion was remote. Crastus was the exception, unlike most of his 'class' he was only interested in results and Schonberg was extremely competent.

"Are you absolutely sure you want me to break the river bank and flood the ditch?" asked Schonberg.

"Yes, as soon as you can in the morning. The water levels inside the curtain walls will not be too high by sun up and your diversion channel that they think is just standard earthworks will stop it rising. I believe they have trusted too much in the level of protection the water will give them. I think they are following Trajan's defence plan to the letter."

"You're kidding me?" interjected Schonberg. "Don't they know it's a fake? Doesn't anybody over there know you wrote it?" The grin on his face was positively wolverine now. He signalled for more wine, his infectious glee evident.

"No." Crastus shrugged. "That fact is known only to a small select band of officers, loyalists to a man. Five years ago, I planted that document in the palace library here in the hope that, if it came down to it and we would have to lay siege, they would have found it and trusted it."

Leander's look of reproach did not surprise Crastus. He had spent hours in the balloon checking out the details, and Leander had almost begun to think that his commander had second sight. Now, all of those insights were revealed as being planned more than five years ago as an elaborate trap and the Pretender's forces had swallowed it completely.

"We proceed with the plan as discussed then?" asked Schonberg as he prepared to take his leave.

"Of a certainty – we'll attack as planned once your diversionary ditch has worked its charm. As soon as we are inside one fortress, we'll give them chance to surrender or withdraw. As agreed, don't reinforce your eastern flank. We must give them an apparent way out. After all, the legions always need recruits!"

The two generals grinned at each other. Schonberg saluted and left as abruptly as he had arrived. Crastus turned to Leander, still grinning.

"I told you; learning comes in many forms and not always from the direction you expected. Let me know when Claudius gets here." With that he turned to his writing table and his letters.

It was only another fifteen minutes before Claudius arrived to report on the dispositions of his Seventh legion, but by now night had fully fallen. In contrast to Crastus' earlier visitor, Claudius was a dapper man whose uniform was pristine. Even so, he was as competent as his opposite number and Crastus was well pleased with the subordinates Valerian thought he had foisted upon him.

Claudius delivered his report in quiet and measured terms. Schonberg had known that his men would be playing an important but relatively passive role in the siege ahead. In contrast, Claudius knew his men would be going into action in the lead and that the outcome depended on him far more than on his Germanic counterpart. As a result, he planned the dispositions of his troops with meticulous care, placing his first and third cohorts on his extreme right up against the Fifth legion and facing AnnMarie. In particular, the centurions of these formations had been quite loud in their objections. Not knowing the plan, they wanted their accustomed position on the honoured left flank. Claudius had almost lost his temper with them, which would have been a very rare occurrence indeed. Now, the man who had created the situation that had caused the aggravation stood in front of him and had just asked if everything was going to plan!

Claudius shrugged. "Yes, fine."

Crastus guessed he had handed several problems to his subordinate but trusted him to resolve them, knowing Claudius wouldn't even mention them.

"The Centurions objected, but we're on schedule. As long as the weather doesn't heat up too much, we'll be ready." As his troops were the ones scheduled for the first attack, it was reasonable for Claudius to worry about the weather which could turn an attack into a disaster. Crastus knew his legion commander well and knew that under the apparent facade of a worrier worked a very sharp soldier's brain. Only the combination of circumstances which had resulted in Claudius being sidelined at Salerno and the unfortunate situation with the Senator's wife, had prevented him from having this command himself. He knew that Claudius, however, was quite happy to let someone else hold the poisoned chalice this time.

As quietly as he had arrived, Claudius left and the camps of the three legions subsided into the normal routine of an army on campaign in enemy territory. Sentries were vigilant while the rest slept. When the sun rose the following morning, the vestiges of the high scattered cloud were fleeing to the east as a stiff breeze blew from inland.

After a hurried breakfast on the north bank, most of the men of the Seventeenth, apart from those on picket duty, were digging hard. The ditch ran from a few yards short of the river bank at its western end and extended eastward as fast as possible. The soil was piled onto a large earthwork rampart on the outside of the ditch. Even as they worked, stripped to their loincloths, the legionnaire's weapons and armour were never more than a few feet away. Their horses grazed, looked after by a few lucky individuals. If the besieged sallied, the legion in infantry formation would be armed and able to give an account of themselves in moments.

No such sally was forthcoming. Just as on the day before, the fortress walls loomed silently over the working men. Other than the occasional sentry, the crenulated top of the wall remained devoid of life.

Around mid-morning, the Herculean task was completed. The further east the diggers progressed, the easier the ground became and the task sped up. The ditch now stretched for nearly three miles, three- quarters of the way around the fortified North bank, fifteen feet wide and six feet deep at its deepest point and still there was little sign of life within the fortresses.

The troops clambered out of the trench they had dug. They checked that there was no equipment or men left behind and the centurions in turn signalled their sections clear. On receipt of the signals, Schonberg gave the go-ahead to his own First Cohort which had hitherto been kept in reserve as a reaction force to protect the rest of his legion. Now, they fell to with a will. In very short order, the end of the ditch approached the edge of the river.

Soon, water seeped through at the bottom edge and the lead centurion bellowed an order. The men left the ditch and retreated to the top of the earthwork behind them. Several large and brave men tied to ropes held by several legionaries moved gingerly out onto the narrow, trembling spit of earth and chopped at the bank itself. Without warning, the bank collapsed and a breach appeared. Water punched through the hole as the now extremely muddy men were pulled to safety. The breach widened by the second until the entire ditch was joined to the river. It took only minutes to fill to a depth of about six feet. The open end of the ditch began to spew water into the open grassland on the eastern flank. Within an hour, the river had found a new course around the fortifications. The water level within the forts wouldn't rise to the level required for the full flood defence.

As requested by Crastus, Schonberg's men had completed the first, passive but crucial step in the subjugation of the Seven Sisters.

Chapter 6 - Rome

Gaius looked bleary eyed at the palace slave who had just woken him from the sleep of the exhausted. Valerian seemed to need little sleep and assumed that his staff needed as little as he did. It must have been after midnight before he had been able to grab a hurried supper and retire. Now, what felt like only minutes later, this poor wretch was shaking him awake and trying to tell him the emperor demanded his presence.

Demanded was the right word. Valerian never asked anything of anybody and the divine right of emperors was alive and well in the court of this particular one. Wearily, Gaius signalled to the mute slave that he understood and swung his legs out of bed. Grabbing a long toga. he made his way out into the corridor. The anxious slave hopped from one foot to the other in agitation so the summons was urgent.

Gaius stalked through the corridors towards the audience in a foul mood. He needed his sleep, for goodness sake! The corridors were silent at this time of night and, to the unobservant, would have appeared deserted. Gaius knew that every twenty paces or so, stationed in shadowed niches, there were Praetorian Guards who would be watching his every move. Ignoring the unseen guards came naturally to a man like Gaius who spent his life within the confines of the palace.

"Gaius! Where the hell are you, Gaius?" The stentorian bellow echoed down the corridors of the palace.

Valerian was in a foul mood. Again.

The chamberlain eventually arrived in Valerian's private audience chamber. Cursing under his breath that the three nubile slaves assigned to keep the emperor busy and his prodigal appetites sated, had obviously not successfully put him in the mood for sleep, he drew himself upright and bowed low, trying desperately to catch his breath.

"There you are!" grunted an exasperated Valerian. "Have you seen these reports from Zampetta? Well, have you?"

"Yes, Sire, but I did not think that they were important enough to disturb you at your repose."

"Did not think? That's right you didn't!" Valerian was working himself into a fit. "Some people in the palace know what's important rather than worrying about whom."

Gaius sighed. Someone on his staff was carrying information and innuendos behind his back. Not that it surprised him. Palaces were like that. They always leaked like a sieve.

"So, your cousin has made it to Zampetta on schedule then."

It was a rhetorical question, Gaius simply waited.

"According to the courier, he not only made it on time but so did his siege train, and the Seventeenth and his first main supply caravan is expected to arrive today as well."

"Well, what do you have to say for yourself?"

"Sire, I don't know what you want me to say. Surely the fact that he is on schedule is good news."

"Bah, where do I find these people? You know dammed well that I want him to be behind schedule not on it. I don't want your people interfering as yet, but I don't want him to have too easy a task either!"

Gaius shrugged off the insult; after all he had been the one who had plotted Valerian's route to the throne not the other way round. Valerian stayed on the throne because of his machinations. He was well aware that Crastus was supposed to succeed in capturing the complex of fortresses but only after the deadline set by Valerian had passed. It was intolerable to the increasingly neurotic emperor that such a prize should still be in the hands of an opposing force fighting a lost cause. It was equally intolerable for a general to be more popular than the emperor himself.

Valerian's stratagem was simple, delay Crastus enough to miss the deadline but not enough to be noticed. Gaius knew his cousin would have reasoned this out and would therefore take counter measures accordingly. As the political dance whirled off into another beat, Gaius found himself intrigued. Which of the dancers would cope and which would fail?

Eventually, Gaius's well used platitudes calmed the spluttering emperor and he watched the man head back to his sleeping quarters and the no doubt welcoming arms of the slaves awaiting him there.

Chapter 7 - Preparations

Crastus clapped his hands and the hubbub among his dining companions died off quickly. Into the silence, Crastus proposed a toast.

"To Emperor Valerian! Long may he rule and Rome prosper!"

It was the patrician's toast, not the more stirring military campaign toast they had expected. Crastus watched, amused, as his subordinate generals and their senior staff exchanged glances whilst responding in kind.

"To work, gentlemen," he said as he signalled the servants hovering just outside the brightly lit centre of the tent. A simple hand signal to the centurion in charge of the guard ensured that after the plates and platters of fruit that was all that remained of the banquet had been removed the servants were themselves ushered out of earshot.

"Schonberg, well done. Good work on the ditch. I still don't believe they didn't anticipate it though." The commander of the Seventeenth nodded in appreciation of the compliment but held his tongue.

"What's the water level inside the fort complex?"

"Less than two feet, and it'll go down further before dawn," replied the big, blonde German.

"Cesca, where are we in regards to the siege engines?"

The senior centurion of the tenth cohort of the Fifth, and the acknowledged expert in the complex engineering of these machines spoke up.

"Local wood supplies are good. We have two full cohorts from both the Fifth and Seventh cutting, squaring and trimming wood and the initial frame construction is underway. We should have two towers competed within three days. The first pair of catapults and ballistae will be ready a day later. After that, each day we'll be able to finish two catapults and two ballistae or be flexible if the plan changes. You would have had two catapults tomorrow, but we have to build the towers first in order to soak them thoroughly."

The concise report elicited smiles of approval all round the table. It would usually take a week longer to produce the equipment Cesca had listed. A couple of them remembered that as former garrison commander in the area, with the Fifth, Crastus along with Maximus and Cesca would have know which copses were the most suitable for siege engine timber. They would have been prepared to cut and destroy them in the event of a besieging army approaching. It was obvious to these men that the legion commanders inside the city had either not bothered or not had time to carry out the same surveys, or timber felling.

The wolfs-head grin was back on Crastus's face.

"You lucky . . ." said Claudius, alone among the officers present with high enough prestige and rank to tease his boss.

"I know, I know, but if they make a mistake, I'll take advantage" said Crastus in his self-depreciating way. "I don't understand why they are so quiet in there. Any ideas?"

"I don't either," replied Claudius, serious now. "If you or I or even Schonberg here," a quick smile to show no malice intended, "was in charge, we wouldn't be. Spoiling raids on the Seventeenth's earthworks would have been a must, as would movement out towards the coast to try and come round behind us with some raiding force."

"We have to assume that they intend to sit behind those walls and let us come to them. Not the way we would have done it, but maybe their command structure was more badly damaged in the retreat from Salerno than we realise. Nevertheless, assume nothing, guard against other possibilities also..

"As soon as the catapults and ballistae are ready I want them in place in front of AnnMarie. I want them to think that we are walking into their trap and attacking the main wall as planned by the Seventh. Four days from now, I want the bombardment to begin. At the same time, get the towers assembled and approaches marked out as if we are going to use them against Isabelle. How long do you think before your men would have a usable breach?" The question was directed at Claudius.

"Two days, tops. If the walls are as weak as we think they are, we should have the tops off in a day and the pounding of the facing stones to drop the wall would only take another day. If they are stronger than we think then, another day at most. Can I use the Sky Nest tomorrow to walk my catapult teams through the plan?"

Crastus nodded - he didn't need to go up again at this point. After all, he knew the layout of the complex like the back of his hand. What Claudius had requested only made sense.

"Actas, any sign of the Eleventh?" he asked.

"Nothing. My men are riding around and spearing daisies," said the quiet auxiliary commander.

A round of low chuckles sounded as the men responded to the cavalryman's reference to the traditional test of skill used to initiate recruits into his light cavalry.

"There'll be work aplenty for you yet," Crastus assured him. "Right, gentlemen, so far the campaign is going perfectly to plan. In no more than six or at most seven days time, the Seventh will begin to demonstrate against both Isabelle and AnnMarie. As we rehearsed on the sand tables back in Rome they must be drawn into reinforcing both so those demonstrations will need to be convincing. As soon as night falls, my mountain boys will go up the corner of AnnMarie where the walls are cracked and will take the defenders from behind. Any questions?"

As usual there were none and before Crastus nodded dismissal he reminded them that the sand table model would be reassembled here within two days.

Left alone, he began to peruse the reports from Rome the dispatch rider had brought in just before the meal began. As he read, the feeling of foreboding began to grow again. Whilst everything in front of him seemed clear and simple, things behind seemed to be getting murkier and darker still.

Chapter 8 - AnnMarie

The day dawned clear. Even before the sun had fully cleared the horizon, the deep twang of the first of the catapults as it released followed a few seconds by the louder thud as the boulder hit the walls of AnnMarie echoed across the field. This was always the hardest time for all concerned. For the catapult and ballistae crews, it was hard, back-breaking work. For the troops massed, it was nerve wracking watching as they knew they would be sent into the attack as soon as the walls were breached. For the defenders, equally so. Not only were they caught in a fixed position with no way of responding, most of their own catapults had been left behind in the flight from Salerno. They could only await the attack, but they were also in direct danger.

After a couple of hours, the monotonous noise redoubled as the newly built third and forth catapults were brought into position and added their firepower to their brothers. As promised by Cesca, the previous day had seen the crenulations at the top of the wall broken down and already the neat facing stones were battered to the point that the wall looked positively scabrous.

The newer tread wheel catapults were so much more powerful than the simpler designs the walls had been built to resist that, by lunch time, there appeared to be a slight swaying to the wall whenever a really accurate shot hit. The bundles of arrows fired from the four ballistae were keeping the heads of the defenders well and truly down. The pounding continued unabated. The swaying motion at the top of the wall was soon more noticeable than before.

"Not long now," said Crastus as he and Leander swung precariously seventy feet above the ground in the basket of the Sky Nest. The breeze today was quite fresh and, as a result, the basket's motion was enough to make Leander feel queasy. Crastus as ever was giving the impression that it was not bothering him at all. Leander was still unable to fathom whether his commander was truly impervious to such concerns or simply very good at hiding them.

Leander agreed with his commander and watched as tiny in the distance the three lead cohorts of the Storming Seventh formed up just behind the catapults ready to advance. Obviously from a much closer position, Claudius could see that the fall of the walls was imminent so his trumpets sounded and the three formations of men began to move forward at a measured, but slow, pace. With a resounding crash, one catapult sent its bulky projectile crashing clean through the wall about one third of the way up from the ground. With their support removed, the stones immediately above began to tremble and slowly fall away into the hole. Like a chain reaction the next course of stones began to follow. At a quickening speed the next course of stonework followed; then the next and the next. Within two minutes the whole section of wall crashed and slid down.

As the dust settled, they could see that a one-hundred foot breach had been opened in the wall and the collapsed stonework made a steep and jumbled, but certainly navigable ramp up to it. The attacking troops broke into a loud cheer and not even needing the echoing trumpet calls picked up the pace and charged. The ranks parted as they swarmed around the catapult crews and reformed in front of them. Now the catapults changed to throwing bushels of small rocks into and around the breach to encourage the defenders to keep their heads down. The ballistae were showering the walls to either side with bundles of arrows whose deliberately loose bindings parted in mid flight to achieve the same result. As expected, not all of the defensive fire could be suppressed in this manner. From behind the walls, the couple of fixed small catapults began to fire back. They did not have the range of their larger cousins constructed by Cesca, but their targets were conveniently coming into range of their own free will. A few hardy souls on the wall fired down on the advancing troops, too. From a fixed position and firing downwards, the legionary bow was a lethally accurate weapon. Luckily, the number of defenders firing was low and, although men began to drop here and there along the line, the range was still extreme.

Charging troops have their own momentum, the range was decreasing very quickly and the casualty rate was rising. As the troops approached the foot of the walls and the pile of broken masonry which would provide them entry, the defenders had to expose more and more of themselves to manage the steeper trajectory. The suppressive fire now began to take a toll, too. Similarly, the best archers in the three cohorts had stopped some fifty yards short of the wall, erecting their shields on their integral support legs had begun to add aimed fire over the heads of their comrades in the attack. Even from the distance, it appeared obvious to Leander that the weight of defensive fire was much too light and that Claudius, given different orders, had enough force to at least carry the breach.

Crastus nodded to the signaller behind him and he immediately began to semaphore the withdraw command. Claudius had obviously been waiting for this for no sooner had the flag been raised that the trumpets pealed out the recall. Leander watched with some wonder as the discipline of the legion showed itself pre-eminent. Despite the fact that it was obvious to all of the attacking men that they could take the breach, they still turned in excellent formation and retreated. One lone defender stood on the wall and jeered as they turned. His show of bravado and little sense came to an abrupt end when arrows from three of the archers tore into him. The walls were thereafter silent as the Storming Seventh withdrew out of range, taking their wounded with them.

Although the ground they vacated appeared littered with dead, they were thinly scattered and the casualties were less than Crastus had feared. Spending men on a diversionary attack was not something he did lightly. Motion at the city gate caught his eye and he breathed a sigh of relief as he saw an entire cohort of the defenders march out of the gate and begin to cross the causeway towards AnnMarie. His plan to trick his opposite number into committing too many forces to defend one point was working. The more troops he could eliminate within AnnMarie, the easier the rest of the campaign would go. Tonight would now be, as planned, the pivotal moment for the whole operation.

Estimating there were only two hours of good light, he signalled the winch crew to lower the basket. As soon as it touched down, he leapt nimbly out of the basket followed by Leander. Two other observers immediately jumped into the basket and the winch crew began to haul them aloft. Two legionaries came forward to remove the standard issue gear both had worn to lead the enemy into thinking they were mere observers and quickly re-donned their more highly polished and ceremonial armour that denoted their rank.

"Do you think the plain armour deception works? After all, they know the rulebook, too," said Leander.

"Probably not," said Crastus. "But it does provide an element of doubt for them, doesn't it? Doubt in the mind of the enemy is something to foster whenever possible," he quoted from the general staff handbook all Roman officers had been force-fed for the last three hundred years.

"It's a force multiplier and will help to restrict casualties." Leander dutifully finished off the quotation to show that he was both aware of and appreciative of his commander's teaching.

Despite their height above the battle for the last couple of hours, the dust kicked up by the fighting had still caked them both quite liberally. They doused themselves with water from a strategically placed bucket and after a necessary visit to the latrines returned to the headquarters tents for a light meal while preparing for the evening assault. Standard doctrine from the same handbook said that you started a night attack after midnight when your opponents guard would be at its lowest ebb. Crastus had learned from his own experience that such surprise attacks would stand very little, if any chance of success when the enemy were steeped in the same strategies from the same handbook. As a result, his attack was going to go in straight after nightfall when it was hoped the troops inside would be too busy preparing their main meal to be very alert.

Sure enough, as darkness fell, the defenders saw the new pickets coming forward to replace those who had been on watch for the afternoon stint. With the failing light and well used to the marching camp disciplines employed by all legions across the empire, they failed to notice one crucial fact. The relieved soldiers did not return to the camp. Instead they simply lay down in the grass making them very difficult to spot and wolfed down the packed meal their 'replacements' had brought forward to them. At a single simple stroke the force directly in front of the fortress had been doubled. An hour later in full darkness, the rest of the third cohort crawled, or ran crouched where cover was better, up to and then beyond the line of pickets. The now-rested men joined them.

Silently, the handpicked men, all from the northern region of Italy crept forward. Most were expert climbers, the rest expert archers to a man. They were now being called upon to demonstrate their skills. As with the diversionary assault earlier in the day, about a quarter of the men – the archers – stopped fifty paces short of the wall and holding their bows loosely, prepared to defend their comrades should the alarm be given. Crastus's luck still held good, no such alarm was forthcoming.

The remaining men reached the foot of the wall where the eastern tower of AnnMarie joined the curtain wall which connected the fort to its neighbour, Gabrielle. The very best climbers amongst them began climbing silently upwards. As Crastus had observed, the ground underneath the curtain wall had shifted slightly and the resultant 'heave' had opened cracks in the courses of stonework along the joins between the two structures. The curtain walls had been added about fifty years after the completion of the original fortresses had been built and the tying in had eventually produced the weakness Crastus was attempting to exploit.

With finger and toe holds at relatively even distances apart, it was as simple as walking up a staircase for these men. Forty men under the command of Optio Lucius veered off to their right when they reached the top of the curtain wall whilst the rest of the troops climbed towards the top of the tower. Working quickly, the small unit paid out the ropes they had carried up and other men attached their equipment to it. The swords and shields, muffled by layers of cloth, were quickly hauled up and the men silently armed themselves. Most of the shields were erected in a simple barrier across the width of the wall and along the exposed inside edge to provide cover from any attacking archers. Most of the men held their swords at the ready whilst a few readied their bows.

The very nature of battle meant it was this much smaller force which was spotted first. One of them must have made a slight noise because the alarm cry rang out and was abruptly cut off with a guttural groan as one of the alert archers at ground level slammed an arrow into the unfortunate mans throat. With the alarm given, speed was now the priority rather than silence. Their position would quickly become untenable if the main force did not take the tower and some of the men, despite harsh whispers from their Optio, could not help glancing nervously upwards to check on its progress.

Only seconds after the sentry had given the alarm and paid a heavy price for doing so, the first of the cat-like climbers rolled through the crenulations and, drawing their daggers, advanced on the few remaining confused and now panicky sentries. Unable to carry their heavier weapons with them for fear of noise, they were at a disadvantage when facing the fully armed sentries. The value of surprise was everything. These men had been handpicked for this job and outmatched their luckless opponents in single combat.

The brief but vicious close quarter knife fight took something less than two minutes to complete. In all, it cost them only one dead and two slightly wounded before they controlled the top of the tower. The bodies of eleven sentries littered the cramped platform and, as more and more men clambered over the wall to join their faster comrades, several had already let down the ropes that would both aid their compatriots and haul up their weapons and armour. Quickly equipping themselves, they took stock of their situation.

The stairwell down into the tower was open where it should have been shut and barred from the inside. Although inviting, every time someone showed themselves too close to it an arrow whistled up out of the darkness inside clearly demonstrating that some of the enemy at least were alert. Looking down at the wall towards the earlier breach, they could see that very few sentries were in place there and that these were staring uncertainly at the tower. The centurion in charge quickly detailed a small group to sweep the walls clear with arrows and turned his attention to the inside of the fortress.

Like all fortresses built a couple of hundred or more years ago, the inside had become a small town. Several streets ran the length and breadth of the once clear ground inside the fort. Just as outlined by Crastus in his briefing earlier in the evening, the buildings nearest the walls had been gutted and their walls extended to reach the outer wall. This created a series of interlocking courtyards surrounded by high walls from which the defenders could unleash a devastating fire on any attacking force.

The area immediately behind this boiled with activity as the encamped troops there tried to don their armour, pick up their weapons and douse their cooking fires all at the same time. Shaking his head at the lack of discipline he saw before him, he quickly ordered several of his men to begin shooting randomly down into the crowd below to increase the confusion. Satisfied, he turned as a shout indicated that another group of his men had just rushed the stairs. The sounds of battle raging on the floor below told eloquently of the savagery unfolding in the near darkness.

At this stage, there could be no quarter. His men had to take the tower and block the door from the main body of the fort without delay. The sounds of battle receded as his men fought their way down the staircases inside. Once clear of the tower top itself, the flaws in the three hundred year old design of the fortress began to show. The staircases descended straight from the top to ground level. In a more modern fortress the stairwells would be staggered and fitted with trapdoors that could be pulled or dropped into position to specifically prevent what was happening to the defenders now. With every fibre, he wanted to join his men as they fought their way through the torch lit tower, but he knew his place was to direct the capture and defence of the tower from the top. Crastus had been very explicit to that effect. Soon, the defenders would counter attack and he and his team must be ready for them. Eventually, a breathless legionary reported, his breastplate smeared with blood from his right arm and his helmet knocked askew.

"All upper floors secure, sir. We are almost in control of the ground floor. The tower doors are closed but not yet barred." As if on cue, the deep jarring thud of the door bars dropping into place echoed up the stairwell.

"Well done, lad, now get that arm seen to," said the centurion as the young soldier in front of him finally allowed himself to grimace in pain.

Now, the tables were turned on the defenders, the centurion thought. With his troops controlling the tower top, the highest point within the fortress, the defenders were vulnerable to arrow fire from above. When daylight came, they would also be vulnerable to direct fire from the catapults with the missiles being literally walked onto target by the forward observers stationed with his men. The outer doors of the keep were armoured, and it would take a very large battering ram and a lot of time to breach them – something they were confident the defence had neither of. The firing slits defending them were well manned and the archers stationed there would take a huge toll of any such assault. It would be extremely costly for the defenders to throw him out of this position. Bundles of arrows and bushels of rocks were being hauled up to them and the walls to either side of the tower were swept by arrows from his men. The supply operation would go on unimpeded all through the night. They were inside!

Chapter 9 - Inside

As dawn broke after the long tense night, it was obvious to both sides that the defenders of AnnMarie were in deep trouble. During the night, several assaults on the tower, aimed either at the door or along the walls, had been attempted with no success and many casualties. Just before dawn, a four-pronged attack along the fortress walls, against the door, and along the curtain wall brought the closest fighting yet.

The troops attacking along the breached outer wall were the most vulnerable. Archers stationed outside the fortress could see them silhouetted against the lightening sky, and they could not defend themselves effectively against fire from above and the side. That portion of the attack broke down almost immediately. The attack on the door was similarly fruitless. The doors would not give way to the light battering rams available to the defence and the testudo was bombarded from the tower top until forced to retreat.

The curtain wall attack was pressed home with real vigour by troops from the neighbouring fortress of Gabrielle. The undamaged curtain wall provided cover from the flank so they could drive forward using their shields to the front and top.

Lucius's troops defending this crucial access were almost overwhelmed in the resulting hand-to-hand fighting. Eventually, with over half their number down, supporting fire from the tower top broke the will of the attackers who retreated back to Gabrielle. In an equally determined attack, a small group of defenders managed to scale the tower from the inner wall and three of their number actually made in onto the fighting platform before being cut down.

With daylight, the full force of the attacking legions could be brought into play.

During the night, the catapults had been augmented by another two, as had the ballistae. Brought forward into almost point blank range of the east end of the breach, they could now pour directed fire directly through the breach and into the heart of the defenders. At such short range, they could throw heavier boulders high into the air which crashed down with devastating force onto the walls and men inside. With daylight, the archers on top of the tower were able to sweep the wall on the other side of the breach with withering fire and this position, too, was denied to the defending force. Similarly, the Seventh moved their archers into range of the Western tower and a brisk archery duel ensued preventing the tower force from interfering with the catapult crews. Nevertheless, the shield walls in front of the catapults bristled with arrows which marked just how bitterly the assault was contested.

On two sides of the fort, the outer walls had become no-man's land. Moving in the open within the fort was asking for trouble for over half of the fort's area. The roofs and wall tops of the buildings within the fort were also swept with archery fire. The inner towers were not quite as high as their outer counterparts and as a result were unable to provide effective suppression fire against the occupied tower top.

The three cohorts of the Seventh that had so successfully demonstrated against the fortress on the day before now marched in formation up to the breach. Only an occasional man fell as the defender's fire was so fully suppressed. They poured up the ramp of broken masonry, which would have otherwise been a killing field and, on command from the signals on the tower, split off inside into different directions to attack further key points.

The maze of deliberately constructed high walled courtyards was no longer the trap they were intended it to be. The men in the tower top could direct their comrades to the concealed doorways and stairwells as well as covering the wall tops to clear enemy archers.

The defence became ever more desperate as the area they controlled began to decrease further until they had been split into pockets of resistance where they were hampered by their own numbers. After an hour or so of bitter fighting, most of the troops outside the three towers retreated to the main gatehouse in reasonable order. There, they opened the fortress gates and attempted to cross the causeway back to the city.

The wisdom of assaulting and taking the eastern tower was now confirmed. As soon as they came out of the shelter provided by the inner tower, an arrow storm dropped the retreating troops in windrows on the thin, raised strip of solid ground. A small percentage managed to get all the way to the city gate itself and safety. A few more were able to crouch in the muddy water in the lee side of the causeway and were able to escape that way. The rest were trapped as arrows rained death amongst them.

The bloody work went on for hours but, eventually, the remaining men in the interior of the fortress began to throw down their weapons and surrender. Quickly, they were rounded up and marched out through the breach, across the grassy plain and into the woods beyond. Now, only the three towers remained in enemy hands. Crastus left them alone to allow the tension to build for the defenders.

Although they held strong defensive positions within the towers and their occupation thereof denied a high proportion of the interior of the fortress to the men of the fifth because they could fire down into it; the other side of the coin was more serious. To fire down in such a manner from the tower top would expose them to return fire from the occupied eastern tower. The firing slits on the other floors would give them only limited aiming points. Quickly, the legionnaires built shield walls across the open spaces, two shields high which provided ample protection whilst they went about making good as much of the damage to the interior as they could. The inner towers were poorly provisioned and had no clean water supply. The external western tower, although provisioned against a siege, had not been able to replenish its water supply due to the speed and ferocity of the assault. Nor did they have an easy escape route. They were surrounded by Crastus's troops and could not even access the curtain wall connecting the fort to its neighbour, for reasons of their own, the engineers had connected the curtain wall on that side to the west facing wall about twenty yards short of the tower itself. As a result it was too far away to provide even a risky escape route.

Crastus himself entered the fortress via the breach in the late afternoon. Flying the flag of truce, an officer was immediately sent to the innermost eastern tower. On the agreement of a short truce, Crastus approached and the senior office, a junior tribune from the force inside appeared in the doorway as its hasty barricades were pulled away. The young officer was clearly the worse for wear, his arm was bound to his side and dried blood coated one side of his face. He had evidently been in the thick of the fighting during the early morning and now found himself in command of a desperately trapped force. Nevertheless, his training was still much in evidence as he drew himself up and saluted, albeit with the wrong arm as his right was injured.

"Tribune Sabinus of the Eleventh."

There was a slight gasp and murmurs from the small group of officers behind Crastus. The Eleventh was not supposed to be here. Indeed they had been screening against its possible move south to relieve the garrison. Obviously, their information was somewhat faulty. The Eleventh, or parts thereof, were here now..

Crastus merely smiled, unsurprised He had noted the insignia on some of the captured men. Maximus grinned, too. He was as observant as his commander, maybe the others would learn in time

"Crastus, General, Commander of His Imperial Emperor Valerian's forces investing this fortress." He replied formally and then continued. "Tribune, you know your position is hopeless. You have no water, you have no hope of rescue, you have wounded who need treatment and, come dark, we will float burning fascines around the tower to prevent you attempting to slip away and wade to safety."

He saw the brief crestfallen look pass over the tribunes face at the latter. Obviously, that had been their plan of action. If the young man survived, he would have to learn about negotiations particularly if facing someone of Crastus's stature who also held all of the cards.

Crastus pressed on, "If you surrender now, we will spare your lives and the men will be absorbed into the Fifth and Seventh and given full honours for service. The Emperor has ordered all three formations in rebellion to be disbanded and their eagles retired. Their names will have no part in the Empire's order of battle in the future. All officers from senior Tribune to Commanders are to be treated as traitors and taken in chains to Rome. That I cannot change. You are a lucky man, Sabinus, not to have risen higher yet. All junior officers are to be treated as prisoners of war and entitled to ransom themselves whereupon they will be dispatched to the far corners of the Empire to resume their service. They will be allowed to return after ten years."

Crastus paused to observe the effects of his words upon the young officer before him.

"Decide now or we will storm the tower or simply burn you out."

The ultimatum fell with the weight of absolute sincerity. The terms were harsh, but not so severe as to force them to go on fighting. If there had been an officer of more senior rank present, it might have been different.

Sabinus turned and murmured something to the men behind him, out of sight in the doorway. Upon getting an answer, he turned and faced Crastus again.

"You have us. We will emerge the door in five minutes." He saluted and turned and re-entered the tower and closed the door. From the lack of sound from within, they didn't bother to push the barricades back into place.

Five minutes later, the door at the foot of the tower re-opened and the Tribune led a few dozen men out into the bright sunlit courtyard. They were unarmed and most had bandages about some part of them.

Approaching Crastus, he again saluted and reported himself a prisoner.

"The stretchered wounded are gathered inside the door, fifteen of them. With proper care, most will make it. In their name I ask for fair treatment."

Crastus nodded and immediately his own medical orderlies made for the doorway.

"Why are there so few fit men remaining in your command?"

"Sir, the tower garrison was sent out to fight in the fort proper. The wounded were quartered in the tower for shelter. When you took the rest of the fort, half a dozen men retreated here and barricaded themselves in to protect the wounded. I must ask you to accompany me to the second floor. There is someone you need to see and there is little time."

Crastus raised an eyebrow at this unexpected request but nodded and accompanied by several of his bodyguard followed the young Tribune into the ground floor of the tower.

It was a charnel house. Groaning wounded men lay on stretchers all over the dimly lit room. In one corner, an untidy heap of grotesquely angled and mutilated bodies showed clear evidence that the fighting around the tower had taken a full reaper's toll. He stepped gingerly past the wounded men taking care not to disturb the orderlies that had flooded in as soon as the surrender had been accepted and following his guide made his way up the stairs on the left.

"In here, sir," said Sabinus, gesturing to a windowless small room set back against the outside wall of the tower. The gloom inside was even thicker despite the flickering oil lamps that ringed the room at shoulder height. The figure on the pallet in the middle of the room shifted slightly in a semi-conscious state. The ugly sucking wound in the side of his chest with the remains of two arrows sticking from it seemed to bubble as the man drew a slow, tortured breath. Crastus approached closer, the man had obviously been shot from the side and below. The man's armour was brightly polished but discarded off to one side as someone had obviously tried to save his life. One quick glance at the terrible wound told Crastus that the attempt was futile. The man had at best only minutes left.

Sabinus lifted a lamp closer so that Crastus could look at the man's face. Shock held him still as he absorbed what he was seeing. Lying on the pallet taking his last few breaths was none other than Agrippa, the Pretender's senior commander and commander of the Eleventh Legion itself.

Crastus shook his head sadly; no wonder the young officer at his side had seemed so shaken. Although the two commanders had not served together for years, and circumstances had put them on opposite sides of this brutal civil war, Agrippa had been one of Crastus's earliest friends when they had served together.

"He knew you would come yourself to take our surrender," said Sabinus quietly. "He told me to save the men and to fetch you personally so that he could say goodbye."

The dying man's eyes fluttered half open and tried to focus on the faces above him.

"I'm here old friend." Crastus lifted Agrippa's cold hand in his own.

A ghost of a smile seemed to pass over his face and then with a gurgling rattle Agrippa's chest heaved and then stopped. The hand Crastus let go now flopped to the floor.

Sad that his old friend was gone but at the same time happy that he had at least escaped the fate Valerian would have doled out upon capture, Crastus stood with head bowed in silence for a moment. His bodyguard outside the small room passed the word down the stairs and the news that they had decapitated the fabled Eleventh Legion buzzed through the fortress. Crastus straightened and turned, leaving the room. Descending the stairs, he exited the tower followed by the tribune who must have been Agrippa's aide.

"Your men will be looked after. Once you have had treatment, present yourself at the HQ tent no later than sundown. If you will excuse me, I must deal with your compatriots." Crastus left Sabinus in his wake. Gathering up the colour party, he moved off in the direction of the inner western tower, hoping for a repeat performance.

This time, not even a single officer had survived to make it into the tower. The senior option in command surrendered quicker than had Sabinus. There had only been seven able bodied men in the tower. The two legion's sharpshooters had left the rest strewn dead on the roof as they had tried to help their fellow legionnaires in the body of the fort below during the fighting.

Crastus, completely satisfied with the outcome, made his way over to the final point of resistance: the outer western tower. To his surprise, his presence had not been needed. The men inside had trussed up their commander, a senior Tribune by the unusual name of Postumus, marched out by themselves and laid down their weapons. In front of their somewhat astonished besiegers, they had formed ranks and waited for someone to take charge of them. A fuming Postumus was literally shaking with rage but was bound and helpless.

Crastus was pleased that he had completed the capture of the fortress with no more bloodshed but saddened that he now had a higher ranking captive to send to Rome for what would be a hideous and eventually fatal fate at the hands of an extremely vindictive Emperor.

Signalling Maximus to take charge of the men and detail a section of men to take the captive into custody, Crastus turned and surveyed the damage to the proud AnnMarie.

Apart from the breach in the western outer wall, there had been no major structural damage to the outside of the fortress. A few weeks work of the stonemasons would return the rest of the fort to its previous grandeur; another month or so would restore the wall, too. It had never fallen to assault before. Although they would be able to restore her stonework, her reputation was something else. AnnMarie would never be the same.

Chapter 10 - Plans

As was the custom whenever Crastus was on campaign, and each unit was in close contact, the senior officers gathered at Crastus's tent at nightfall. Some were surprised to see Sabinus in attendance. With his wounds dressed and wearing a clean tunic, the young Tribune looked better if not happier. He sat slightly to one side and glumly listened to the reports of the men around him. Even if his honour had not prevented him breaking his word to Crastus and attempting to escape, his inability to use his right arm would hinder him and the maniple of soldiers waiting outside the tent would stop him.

Crastus was not stupid; he had no intention of revealing his plans in front of the officer from the Eleventh. The opportunity to use him as a go-between at a later stage of the siege required him to be treated with some decorum and was not something to pass up.

Finally, once the reports on the days actions had been completed, confirming that the Fifth and Seventh had suffered fewer than two hundred dead and the same number wounded between them, and that the Seventeenth had had a quiet day as spectators, Crastus turned to Sabinus.

"I think you need your rest more than you need to listen to discussions that will not involve you in any way."

Dismissed in a way that saved face, Sabinus acknowledged the barely concealed order and, draining his wine goblet, saluted Crastus, nodded to the other officers politely and made his way out of the tent where his guards formed up around him and took him off to the prison compound.

"The interrogated prisoners – what have they told us?"

A Tribune from the outer circle of officers now stood. His over-large, pointed nose and his close-set eyes had earned him the nickname 'Gaius, the Rat' as soon as he had joined a serving legion. His quick mind and attention to detail had gained him an intelligence billet and he very quickly developed a knack for interrogation. Unlike most of his brethren in the experienced category, he rarely used force or torture. This had helped to ensure that Crastus's patronage had been extended to him, quickly followed by a transfer into the coveted intelligence billet in the Fifth.

Gaius started almost hesitantly but quickly became more animated in his presentation.

"As we were able to deduce from the presence of young Sabinus there, as well as other prisoners, and his now deceased Commander Agrippa, at least one cohort of the Eleventh was inside the city. In fact, we now know the entire legion is present."

There was a collective grimace at the news. With three legions present in the defence, despite today's success, the job of taking the city, had gotten harder.

"In fact, in taking AnnMarie we have managed to destroy two cohorts of the Eleventh, the other two legions are retained within the city. The Eleventh held five – four now – of the fortresses. Gabrielle is held by two cohorts of the Fourteenth as is Beatrice. Both formations have been brought up to strength by transferring in men from their respective eighth cohorts."

Like all Roman legions, the eighth cohort was used as a mobile replacement depot and tended to receive all of the new recruits so that by the time they reached fighting formations, they had at least some experience. However, after the disaster at Salerno, the likelihood of experienced replacements being available within either legion was remote.

"Each of the other forts is held by one cohort of the Eleventh together with some support troops from their Ninth cohort. They have a reaction force of one cohort from the Eleventh and one each from the Twelfth and Fourteenth, originally under Agrippa, with the rest garrisoning the city walls."

Crastus frowned. Standard doctrine stated that such a reaction force should be derived from a single legion not from a mix of three. The news reinforced his opinion that the force inside the city was not as unified as his own command. The elimination, albeit by fortuitous accident, of the capable commander of the Eleventh had further undermined the command structure. The relatively easy surrender of most of the troops inside AnnMarie earlier in the day had shown less willingness to fight than had been expected to.

"Morale?" asked Crastus

"The prisoners we took were not highly motivated. They know they are the last units fighting for a cause that is already lost. As we saw with the Western tower; give them a way out that means they escape with their liberty without their families paying a price, they will take it. Only the units under control of the strongest officers will stand and fight.

Postumus was a classmate of mine and he didn't expect the mutiny that saw him captured."

A series of rueful grins spread around the circle. Most of those present did not know how they would respond in a similar situation. It had been several hours before the reluctant captive officer had stopped cursing his men long after they had been removed from earshot.

Gaius continued.

"Civilian morale is reportedly very low. They do not want to be in the middle of this. They do not support the Pretender; they have never supported the Pretender. As a result, they need a fair proportion of the reaction force simply to keep a lid on any possible civilian reaction."

"Can we take advantage of that?" asked Leander.

"No, not as yet anyway" replied Gaius.

Crastus intervened before anyone started off down the wrong line. "In any case, we are here to liberate the city and its population. I don't think the Emperor would look favourably if we slaughtered half the merchant class and slaves in the process." Leaning back in his seat, he fixed Gaius with a steady stare. "So, in summary, the Pretender's army find themselves encircled in a fortress complex whose exterior defences have already been breached, with an openly hostile civilian populace?"

"Pretty much."

"Thank you, Gaius. Good work, as always. Now, gentlemen, the quick fall of the whole of AnnMarie means we are ahead of schedule. That at least is good news." The answering grins around the table matched his own. "Has anything that Gaius reported prompted any need to change the plan?" Crastus now threw the meeting open for general discussion. Predictably, it was Schonberg who spoke up first. However, he only piped Claudius by a hair's breadth, the smaller man politely gave way to his more junior but somewhat larger colleague.

"If Claudine is only held by one cohort, are you sure you don't want me to take it out next? My assault teams are just as adept as either of the Fifth or Seventh legions."

The poor man seemed plaintive almost petulant as if he had not yet been allowed to play.

"Don't worry," Crastus replied. "Your turn will come. We want to keep them thinking their line of retreat is open on your side of the river. Besides, it would take a long time to transfer the heavy equipment over the river to you."

Schonberg subsided with bad grace. He couldn't win the argument. He had been trying to ever since he had met up with the other two legions and had first heard Crastus's plan. Crastus wanted to retain as much of the fighting capability of the opposing legions as possible for future use in the provinces many of which were crying out for reinforcements. The five years of constant civil war had taken their toll on the fighting strength of most of the legions and had eaten into the available pool of recruits.

Schonberg was only focused on the near term objective of reducing the Seven Sisters. Crastus was taking a longer view, even if the Emperor would have been happy to annihilate those inside the complex.

Claudius spoke up into the resulting silence.

"Are you sure that Dominique is the next target? I know that's the plan, but I think that Gabrielle would be more easily taken despite the fact that it has more defenders."

"I know Dominique's walls are higher and the river protects one wall, and Claudine can provide enfilading fire along part of the front wall. If we take it, we open up Claudine to attack from all sides, isolate Isabelle and threaten the city itself. Gabrielle and Beatrice are the only close-linked forts with the covered archways between them. They can reinforce each other very easily. We must reduce the main forts south of them before we attempt to crack that particular nut. "

"Their defensive plan invests everything in holding the landward fortresses. They have lost AnnMarie and they dare not lose Isabelle. We have to make them assume that Isabelle is the next target. Once Dominique falls, it becomes only a matter of time."

Chapter 11 - Dominique

Overnight, the sentries within AnnMarie had heard and occasionally glimpsed troop movements into their nearest neighbour, Isabelle. Virtually all of the movement was into the fort and, as they were under orders not to attempt to interdict these movements, they had been allowed to continue unmolested. After all, the overall plan was to allow Isabelle to become a pocket and, as far as the high command were concerned, the more men within the pocket the better. If their opponents really thought that Isabelle was going to be the target, even better when the real blow fell somewhere else.

Dawns showed the defenders their error. During the night, they had clearly heard the besiegers moving their heavy equipment around. Whilst they had heard equipment being moved into position opposite Isabelle, they had not heard the re-greased axles as the catapults had been moved to their real positions further up the line facing Dominique. Crastus's and Claudius's uncanny ability to perform sleight of hand tricks on the battlefield had paid off yet again. Dominique had not been reinforced and in daylight any attempt to do so would be suicidal. All of the approach causeways were within range of either the ballistae or even worse in direct range from the walls of AnnMarie. The newly reinforced troops in their neighbouring fort were almost as impotent as the troops in the city. There was no direct causeway link between the forts. They would have to run the gauntlet twice, once to return to the city, and once back out to Dominique. Even if the order for such a manoeuvre was given, it would be doubtful whether the men would obey.

A short section of the fortress wall adjoining the Western tower as well as the tower top itself would be able to provide enfilading fire. The curtain wall connecting the two would be able to do so, too. With no gate into either fortress, any troops would be left exposed to covering fire and unable to retreat quickly if the need arose. The main purpose of the curtain walls, after all, had been to retain the now receding flood waters as the bulwark of the inner defences. The overall weakness of this design was now exposed. Dominique's defenders were on their own until nightfall at the earliest, if not for longer.

The Seventh legion was drawn up facing the blank wall of the fortress. They were a very impressive sight. Five full cohorts were stretched across a shallow five-hundred yard arc facing Dominique. They would funnel in to assault the whole length of the wall. Two further cohorts were arrayed behind the central three cohorts both as reserves and to provide a reaction and exploitation force. Behind them were the specialist troops and behind them the horse holders. The Fifth were a true cavalry outfit whereas the Seventh was a mainly mounted infantry unit. They would ride to battle but fight on foot. The front ranks carried a myriad of scaling ladders, ropes and grappling hooks. Some even had spikes fastened to the fronts of their boots and claw type gauntlets so that they could directly scale the weathered stone of the walls using the crevices between the stones.

From the height afforded by the sky nest, Crastus could see the magnificent sight of the full panoply of a legion about to go into battle arrayed before him. Everything seemed ready. Within AnnMarie as many as possible of the two cohorts of the Fifth who now garrisoned the captured fort lined the walls, ready to attempt to suppress fire from Isabelle if they could and to cover the causeways to prevent reinforcement from, or retreat to, the city.

Crastus gave the signal.

The ever-alert Claudius, seeing the signaller start the sequence that would order the attack ordered his trumpeters to blow the attack call even before Crastus's flag man had finished. The trumpets pealed in the distance and from the basket it looked a sand table exercise as the blocks of men began to move forwards.

The catapult arms clanged forward against their stops and bushels of small rocks began to rain onto the tops of the wall and the towers to force the defenders to keep their heads down. On the inland flanks, the ballistae were dividing their fire. Covering both the Eastern tower of Dominique and the closest corner of Isabelle, whole sheaves of arrows plunged upwards and then down onto their targets. Being hit by such an attack often meant taking multiple arrows, so it was wise to keep under cover.

Crastus had only eight ballistae and eight catapults available to him. Each took about five minutes to reload with their bundles of missiles and, even with staggered fire, there was at least thirty seconds for the archers to pop up, fire a few arrows and duck back into cover. Nevertheless, the barrage did disrupt the covering fire and cause a slow trickle of casualties. The defender's junior officers, forced to expose themselves more in order to point out the targets to the archers, suffered disproportionately more.

Crastus was well aware of the limitations imposed by his lack of numbers in terms of heavy equipment. He had no choice but to attack given the timetable imposed on him by Valerian, so had modified his plans with Claudius' help to take this into account. AnnMarie had been expected to hold out longer and therefore more heavy equipment would have been available to screen the attack on Dominique. The momentum of the attack had to be kept going. Success was as it had always been, a force multiplier. As a result, the two wing cohorts, one on the river bank; the other almost overlapping in front of Isabelle, had advanced only a couple of hundred yards or so into extreme range before halting. They would take no part in the direct assault on Dominique. Instead, they began to provide galling fire against Claudine on one wing where the river narrowed to plunge through the passage between the forts and Isabelle on the other.

The central three cohorts, together with the two massed behind them, continued to advance on a narrowing front that led all of them into the area directly in front of Dominique. The closer they got to the foot of the wall, the more accurate the defenders became. Men began to fall in increasing numbers. The defensive fire was much more intense than had been faced in the diversionary attack against AnnMarie a mere forty-eight hours ago. There were more defenders here and the wall top was unbroken so they had more cover, as well. Again, at the correct distance, the sharpshooters stopped their advance and, erecting their shields, began to add their arrows to the weight of covering fire.

The rain of arrows and the showers of small rocks thrown by the catapults and ballistae as well as the aimed fire from the sharpshooters looked at close distance to be overwhelming and continuous. Both Claudius from close up and Crastus from the height advantage of the sky nest knew better.

There was a good tactician in charge within Dominique and as soon as the sharpshooters deployed, the few hidden catapults inside the fort began to bombard their positions with incendiaries known as Greek fire. These did not have to be aimed particularly well as, on impact, the burning liquid sprayed out for several feet in all directions. Crastus grimaced at the sight. He hated the use of Greek fire against any target, let alone men, especially his own. It was the work of minutes to neutralize the sharpshooters' effect on the battle and the catapults began to fire on the follow up formations as they shifted targets. The lead men of the attacking cohorts had by now reached the foot of the un-ditched wall and the first ladders were being erected even as the grapple men began to swirl the hooks around their heads, ready to cast. The climbers launched themselves at the wall and began to scramble up. The prongs on their feet were very effective as, over the years, the cracks had widened. They made excellent progress and were well ahead of their comrades until halfway up they found that, invisible from the ground, the cracks had been filled and they came to a halt.

At this point the defenders struck. Momentarily heedless of casualties, they rose and tipped large pots of oil down on the climbers. Most lost their grip and fell into the press of men below. The rest, trapped, unable to climb and with the oil drenched stones around them unable to descend, were easily picked off from the enfilading arrow slits of the towers at each end. None of the climbers made it to the top. Claudius seethed with frustration as he watched his men fall to no avail; one leg of the assault was lost. The grapple men were finding difficulty as well. Generations of wear had worn the stones on the parapet smooth making it difficult for the hooks on the grapples to get a purchase. The defenders were quick to reach any grapple that did catch, throwing them back over the wall. Very quickly, it became apparent that they, too, were futile in this attack. That left only the ladder crews.

The unwieldy long wooden ladders were erected against the walls and men began to swarm up them in single file. With much of the defenders attention focused on the other attacking groups, only some of the ladders were pushed away adding the falling weight of their men to the struggling mass below. The rest of the ladders remained in place and the lead man on each arrived at the top.

It was not a good place to be the first man that day. In two ranks of three on the inward edge of the parapet, the defending archers waited, one rank standing, and one kneeling. As soon as the torso of the climbers cleared the parapet the first rank of archers fired. At point blank range, they didn't miss. As the body plunged past the next man, it was his turn to reach the top. As soon as he did, the second rank fired. Same result. By then, the first rank was ready again. On some of the ladders, the riddled corpses of the legionnaires did not fall free but, pivoting at the knee, crashed down onto the next man and remained tangled by the legs. This jammed the ladder, preventing the men on it climbing higher.

On a few ladders, men managed to see what was happening above them or elsewhere and swung their shields into place before going over the top of the parapet. This wasn't always enough as often the arrows would be driven through the shields, so short was the range.

One particularly enterprising attacker threw himself bodily into the ranks of archers facing him and, although riddled with arrows in the process, allowed two or three of the men following him to get to the top of the wall unmolested. They were then able to distract and divide the attention of the adjacent groups of defenders allowing the neighbouring ladder men to reach the parapet. A truly vicious hand to hand melee now ensued as more and more of the attackers reached the top of the wall and struggled to expand the lodgements.

Men from both sides fought with a savagery rarely seen. The stones that made up the walkway behind the parapet ran with blood, and became increasingly slippery. Bodies, not always dead, plummeted down in a steady rain on both sides of the wall. Although some of the small footholds managed to merge, others were unable to do so.

Claudius from close up to the battle and Crastus from the hanging basket could both see that the attack was not succeeding in sufficient force to carry the day. Already, the tower crews were peppering the ladders and more than half were clogged with bodies. Their minds made up, almost at the same instant they signalled the recall. The argument would rage for months as to who had actually signalled first, although the official history would later claim that Claudius was simply obeying his commander's orders.

The three lead cohorts of the Seventh, badly savaged in the attack, began to retreat, holding up their shields to provide cover as they helped their wounded comrades along, eventually limping out of range.

For the poor brave souls who had made it to the top of the wall, there would be no retreat and with most of their number dead or wounded the few survivors had no option but to surrender.

There was no room for doubt; Crastus's army had suffered a severe rebuff if not a defeat.

Chapter 12 - Wounds

Following the rebuff from the walls of Dominique, Crastus's army recoiled and in places almost convulsed. Rumours spread through the ranks that the campaign would now be abandoned, that a large force was marching from the north to relieve the defenders, and finally, most damaging of all, on Crastus's orders, the Seventh was being sacrificed to protect his own command. A Roman legion was a considerable war machine when things went well, but was demonstrating yet again how fragile it was when things went awry.

Although all of the senior officers were used to the way defeatist rumours would swell after a reverse such as the one just suffered, the sheer ferocity of some of them caught Claudius's staff by surprise. It was early evening before full order had been restored and Claudius was able to report to Crastus's tent for the post mortem.

Crastus had, during the afternoon and early evening, received preliminary reports but was awaiting a final accounting. He expected his second in command to be upset, even livid at the result of the morning's debacle, but even he was unprepared for the purple faced rage on Claudius's face when he eventually arrived.

He stormed into the tent and grabbed the nearest goblet and drained it with one gulp.

"We were too dammed complacent, Crastus!" He stormed on without a pause. "Just because AnnMarie fell so easily, we should not have assumed that the rest would follow like a house of cards!"

He paused for breath, his anger directed at events and the difficult business of the afternoon rather than at any individual, especially not his commander.

"We need more time to bombard the walls before we try an assault like that again. We have to reduce the cover available to them. I knew those bloody crampons were too gimmicky. They didn't work for Caesar at Alesia, and they sodding well didn't work today. I don't think the centurion who proposed them will survive the night with his wounds. Good job, if he lives, I'll have him castrated!"

"We lost over five-hundred good men today with a half-cocked, half-brained, half-hearted attack and I'm not wasting any more of my men on such affairs again!"

Crastus had already seen the reports and knew the casualty figures, some of the officers present knew that they were going to be bad but winced at the scale of the setback.

Schonberg surprised everyone with the possible exception of Crastus himself, by moving forward and wrapping a huge arm around the still seething commander of the Seventh's shoulder and handing him another goblet of well watered wine. Crastus, patient as ever, waited for his second in command to gain an element of control before responding.

"I agree."

Claudius paused with the goblet half way to his lips and looked askance at his commander.

"We thought that we could steamroll over them with the momentum of capturing AnnMarie. In that we were wrong. I watched your attacking troops. We could have asked nothing more of them, but I fear they could have asked more of us."

Such a bold acceptance of error did not surprise those present who had been with Crastus for years, but some of the officers newer to his ways were surprised by the candour.

"The question now is not so much what we did wrong, but what do we now to finish the job."

All of the men present looked at Crastus. They had all witnessed or been in some way involved with the failed assault and were looking to their commander for inspiration just as he was looking at them for it too. Schonberg was the first to speak.

"Do we continue to attack Dominique or do we switch targets?"

"No, my friend, we will continue with the plan as it stands. Dominique must fall next otherwise they will be able to redeploy the troops from Isabelle which we want to leave bottled up."

Claudius stepped in

"If Dominique must be taken next, and I agree with that by the way, then the next assault must come after preparation. We must reduce the tops of the walls so that they can't mousetrap my assault troops again. I would like to use the black powder to blast through the wall too."

"No, Claudius, that we cannot do. We already have a large breach in AnnMarie and the stone masons will have their work repairing that before the Emperor arrives. The newer model catapults are so much more powerful that all of this type of fortification within the empire is vulnerable. That is information we want to keep close. When Valerian arrives, he will be accompanied by many foreign ambassadors. He will not want to be holding court in a set of ruins that clearly show the empire's weaknesses. One breach can be repaired in time, more than one possibly, three definitely not."

The relatively long speech from Crastus brought them up short; they were reminded that the war they fought had more long term implications than simply eliminating the remnants of the Pretender's army.

Claudius shrugged; he was as sensitive to the politics of the situation as his commander, by bringing it up himself he had prevented any of the junior officers present feeling stung by the rebuke. The twinkle in Crastus's eyes as he watched his second-in-command confirmed to Claudius that Crastus knew exactly what Claudius had done. A slight, almost imperceptible nod was exchanged between them, acknowledging their joint mastery.

"Right, gentlemen, taking Dominique traps a large proportion of our opponents in Isabelle, opens up the river to us, isolates Claudine and threatens the city itself directly for the first time. It will present the commanders of the Twelfth and Fourteenth with more problems than they have resources to solve. In three days, I want to see a fully worked up plan of attack that removes any chance of repeating the failure of today. Let's manoeuvre and keep them off balance. Let them think we are attacking in several different places. In the mean time, let's spread the catapults out and take the crenulations and parapet off the top of the walls on both Dominique and Isabelle."

"Confusion to the Enemy! Victory!"

Crastus finished with the familiar toast and, as his officers responded, he wondered just how many more men he would be sending to their deaths in four or five day's time.

Chapter 13 - Tomorrow

"Gentlemen, let's just go over the plan one more time. There must be no mistakes tomorrow."

Crastus called the late night conference to order and looked round the half-circle the faces on the other side of the sand table. In the flickering light of the torches above, the small scale replica of the fortress complex set on the sand table looked more menacing still than the reality a mile away, outside the tent.

Since the capture of AnnMarie and the abortive attempt on Dominique, there had been no attempt at counter attack by the besieged legions. This had surprised many of those present who knew their opponents quite well through the collegiate system of the Roman army, but Crastus had not expected any such move in force. He had arrayed his forces to deal with any eventuality, but remained confident that those eventualities would not arise.

"We'll do this by the numbers. It's complex compared to the other manoeuvres we have carried out here. Leander, call out the count please."

Slightly taken aback that his commander wasn't going to be doing it himself he realized that Crastus wanted to keep his mind clear to spot any weaknesses in the overall scheme, Leander complied.

"One."

Schonberg took a half pace forwards and picking up the slender pointer began.

"My right flank, will demonstrate against Claudine at its exposed northern corner tower where the other fortresses cannot support it."

"Two."

Schonberg stepped back and Maximus, acting for Crastus so that Crastus could remain in an overview position stepped forward and, picking up the pointer, tapped on the model at the junction where the walls of Gabrielle reached the river.

"The right hand cohort of the Fifth will make a determined small scale attack on the river tower of Gabrielle as if we are attempting to take the River Gate Wall or blow the sluice gates. The boxes of black powder we will carry will be dummies, not explosives. We do not wish to blow the gates but rather to draw their skilled engineers to us and, if possible, eliminate or at least maul them.

"Three."

Maximus continued.

"Elements of the First and Third cohorts of the Fifth, will commence firing on Isabelle and Gabrielle from the walls and towers of AnnMarie providing harassing fire as if to cover an assault on either. With luck, this will draw forces away from more important positions."

"Four."

Claudius now took centre stage.

"The catapults attached to the Seventh will finish knocking the wall tops down on Dominique in order to remove the cover there for the defenders archers. My skirmishers, reinforced by my best archers, will also start harassing Isabelle and Dominique in order to get them to keep their heads down as far as possible."

"Five."

Schonberg again stepped up.

"My diversionary attack will stop and the troops involved will mount and head off in the direction of the upstream ford as if they are moving to reinforce Claudius. As soon as they are out of sight of the fortresses, most will stop. A small group will continue, dragging brush to simulate the whole group. The remainder will then infiltrate back to their start positions to be ready to face a counter-attack at the apparent weak point in my lines." The grin on his face was infectious; they all knew he really wanted his opponents to come out and face him so he could cut them to pieces.

"Six."

Schonberg retained control of the pointer and moved round to the left of the model.

"My right hand two cohorts will demonstrate against Beatrice as if to support the Fifth's attack on the river wall."

Crastus broke in, signalling Leander to pause.

"At this point, what do we want them to think?"

"That we're going to attack either Isabelle or Dominique, but they are not sure which, everything else is a feint."

Claudius was a lot happier with this sort of detailed planning, he was known for it is his own right, having pulled off several brilliant set piece manoeuvres of this type in his career. He tended to look down his patrician nose at the more straightforward approach that Crastus preferred.

"What do we want them to do, apart from fall into Schonberg's trap?"

"Reinforce Dominique and/or Isabelle." Maximus spoke up.

"Not quite, Maximus. We want them to be ready to reinforce but still unsure as to which is our target. Therefore they will not commit their reserves to running the gauntlet of fire from AnnMarie until they are sure. When they are sure, we want them to be wrong. Continue."

"Seven."

Maximus stepped back up, tapping on the miniature of AnnMarie.

"The catapults we have constructed within AnnMarie will now commence firing at Isabelle, using the new bombs to create confusion within Isabelle and begin the process of convincing them that that is our point of attack."

Cesca intervened for the first time.

"We still have not solved the fusing problem with the black powder bombs. Often, the fuse ignites the bomb too soon, and just as often does not explode at all. So we are going to try a new trick which has been working well in practice. Three of the catapults will be throwing the bombs with unlit fuses. A few seconds later the forth will throw an incendiary. When the first three projectiles burst on impact the powder should settle over quite a large area and the flaming shot should ignite it all."

They all inwardly shuddered at the thought of the fiery carnage that could ensue from such tactics.

"Eight."

Claudius resumed the narrative.

"The catapults on the right of my section will switch aim point over to Isabelle increasing the rate fire in the process."

"Nine."

"The remainder of the Fifth will now draw up as if they are ready to attack the Eastern exposed flank of Isabelle and troops inside of AnnMarie will appear to be readying to attack along the curtain wall. Meanwhile, Schonberg's diversionary troops will have crossed the ford and will appear to be approaching the rear of our siege lines to reinforce Claudius's attack on Isabelle."

"Ten."

"The troops attacking Gabrielle and Beatrice will fall back, hopefully having caused casualties or at least drawn the attention of the engineering corps from Zampetta."

"Eleven."

Claudius remained on centre stage; his Seventh were ready to avenge the defeat of five days ago.

"The defenders should now be convinced that our attack on Isabelle is imminent so their reserves should sortie from the city to reinforce Isabelle."

"At that point, the troops inside AnnMarie, reinforced by the Fifth's Eighth Cohort which is moving as we speak under cover of darkness, will turn the reinforcement into a gauntlet and cause as many casualties as possible. The catapults inside will increase their rate of fire and concentrate on the area just inside the gate house at Isabelle. Once inside, the survivors should be too disorganised to venture out for some time"

"Twelve."

"The bulk of the Seventh, having remained unengaged and concealed, will now assault Dominique concentrating on the West tower and wall near the river, away from any spoiling fire from Isabelle. In the mean time, Schonberg's two right hand cohorts will resume demonstrating against Claudine to prevent them from being able to harass my flank. That's assuming, of course, that the Seventeenth haven't drawn them out and destroyed them in the mean time. By late afternoon, Dominique should be ours and a fair proportion of their troops should be isolated in Isabelle, where under potential attack from three sides they cannot hope to influence the fight any further, certainly not by escaping back to the city."

"Excellent, gentlemen; now contingencies?"

Leander, who other than keeping count had been silent throughout, piped up.

"What happens if they don't reinforce Isabelle?"

"Good question. It unfortunately means we won't have as many men trapped in Isabelle as we want, but the rest of the plan continues. If they reinforce Dominique, then we will have more work to do in taking that one," said Claudius. With a thoughtful look on his face, he continued.

"In that case, let's bring the towers up facing Isabelle on its right flank so that we can turn them and use them as a backup assault route against Dominique. Schonberg, could you make your diversionary force slightly bigger so that they approach directly behind the towers ready to assist in their movement?"

Schonberg nodded, Crastus was pleased to see his staff thinking and acting in this way. The anger and glum faces following the setback five days ago had been completely replaced within his staff team by the professionalism he expected.

"What happens if my team gains a foothold on the river wall?" asked Maximus.

"Place the dummy explosives and guard the position. Only give ground and retreat if attacked with overwhelming force.

The river wall is a distraction only; it's not worth sacrificing lives over at this stage."

"Is the plan rigid?"

"No, some steps may be taken out of sequence if any of the diversionary forces are suffering too high a casualty rate if they have already achieved their objectives. If so, I'll pull them back early – so watch for that – don't anticipate the signals."

"Where will you be?"

"I'll be in the Sky Nest; control will emanate from there. We will set up a dummy command post facing Isabelle, so acknowledge but otherwise ignore all signals from there."

The dummy command post was one of Claudius's favourite tricks. However, Crastus knew that the ground wasn't particularly suitable for that site, and that there were sure to be officers on the other side who knew of his preference for height over the battlefield. Still, indulging Claudius in this respect would not hurt and keeping his second-in-command on side was worth the minimal expenditure of effort involved.

"Any more questions gentlemen? No? Right to bed; we attack straight after first light in the morning. This time, we will not fail."

One by one, the others filed out, Claudius pausing to check some detail on the model against his own memory. The two stood in silent contemplation of the model for a few minutes, each lost in their own thoughts. Finally, with a nod Claudius withdrew. Crastus stared at the model for some time before following his own instructions.

Chapter 14 - Dominique

By the time the sun peeked above the horizon and the predawn murkiness gave way, Crastus and Leander had already been aloft in the Sky Nest for nearly an hour. Having seen nothing surprising or unexpected within the besieged fortress city, Crastus gave the go ahead to Leander.

"Signal Schonberg One," said Leander to one of the two flagmen who shared their perch, tension obvious in his voice.

One of the early decisions agreed had been to only use flag signals and gallopers, not the usual trumpet calls. Their own troops were used to being given orders by trumpet call. In this case, Crastus wanted to hear the opponent's calls. As always in a civil war, both sides had learned from the same manual of calls and therefore this would give him some advance warning of the enemy reaction without giving away their own. Leander was beginning to appreciate just how hard Crastus would work to achieve the smallest advantage and minimise his own casualties.

In the distance, Schonberg's First and Second cohorts could be seen forming up into ordered assault ranks on the earthworks behind their ditch. Meanwhile, the plank bridges were being run across the ditch and soon the formations broke rank to cross and then reformed. At the standard legion walk they began to advance. They seemed to be in no hurry, but there again they weren't. It was obviously a feint and it was equally obvious that Schonberg and Crastus wanted their opponents to think so, too. Alarm calls rang out within Claudine and were quickly echoed within Zampetta and the other fortresses. Crastus's entire force had breakfasted in the hour before dawn and by the loud response to an obvious feint it was quickly clear that this was something the defenders had been denied the chance to do. Another little advantage built into the attacker's planning process.

As the attacking force reached their designated ranging line, they split into two groups. The better archers planted their shields, unlimbered their bows and began to shower the tops of the walls and towers with arrows. The other troops proceeded to a line approximately fifty paces further and also planted their shields and this time hunkered down behind them. This made themselves unattractive targets to the archers on the walls who were also trying to avoid being hit from the harassing fire.

"Good, signal Maximus Two," said Crastus quietly to the flagman on the other side of the basket.

On their far right, the Seventh cohort of Crastus's own Fighting Fifth began moving forwards towards the juncture between Gabrielle and the river wall above the giant closed sluice gates. As soon as they began their running advance towards the supposed weak point, more alarm calls sounded within the city. To the defenders, it looked like this was a deliberate attempt to remove their water defence from the equation and, as such, was more serious than Schonberg's feint at the other end of the complex. Within the city, the engineering core was quickly assembled and within minutes was marching out of the city via the nearest gate and into Gabrielle.

This was the part of the plan Crastus disliked the most. His Seventh cohort was going to take more casualties than any of the other diversionary forces as they had to convince the troops facing them that it was a real assault.

"Signal Maximus Three," he said even as the first casualties on the right flank began to drop from the defensive fire.

The waiting troops within AnnMarie began to join in, a heavy arrow storm sweeping the walls of Isabelle and Gabrielle and the exposed parts of the interior of Isabelle as the next phase of the plan unfolded. The arrow storm on Gabrielle was simply to prevent too many of the defenders concentrating on the river side attack whilst the Isabelle attack was the start of that feint. This time, his own troops were under cover and should not take too many casualties.

"Signal Claudius Four."

The catapults massed behind the front line of the Seventh began their carefully orchestrated assault on the walls of Dominique. Unlike in the earlier bombardments of both AnnMarie and Dominique, this was meticulously aimed fire. Each set of catapults aimed at the buttresses alongside the crenulations on the very top of the wall. The intention was simply to demolish these, and these only so as to reduce the cover available on the outer edge of the wall to eliminate the defenders ability to cut down the attackers without exposing themselves. It did not take them long to get the range and soon the wall top began to look like a moth eaten cloth.

"Signal Schonberg Five."

Over on the other bank of the river, the attacking cohorts began to withdraw. It was a typically ordered process as the advanced troops retired by sections about ten paces and stopped allowing the next section to do the same. As they reached a point just past the line of archers, the archers joined their retreating comrades. As soon as they were all out of effective range of the fortress, they picked up the pace and doubled back over the plank bridges and on over the earthworks. A scattering of guards retrieved the bridges and took up sentry positions. Very soon afterwards, a large cloud of dust signalled to all observers, friendly or not, that the two attacking units were now riding off. The direction of the movement was soon apparent as well, towards the ford just two miles upstream.

"Signal Schonberg Six."

It was very difficult to observe the far right of Schonberg's force from the Sky Nest with the bulk of the forts and the city itself in the way. Crastus had debated having the platform height increased but had decided against it. This would be the only phase of the plan he could not fully observe and, the higher he took the platform, the more time it would take to descend and re-ascend to send or receive more complex messages than the flag system allowed for. Nevertheless, the sudden increase in noise from that direction informed Crastus almost as much as direct line of sight would have done. The ever dependable Maximus, who was closely watching the progress of his right hand cohort, quickly signalled by flag *Flank, fine* which allayed any fears that the right wing feints were going anything other than as planned.

Now the commander paused. It was time to let the tension build for the defenders and allow the catapults firing on Dominique to complete their work. Ordering a descent, Crastus waited impatiently for the Sky Nest to complete its earthward journey. Almost on cue as he jumped down from the platform, three gallopers rode up; two with the Seventh's banners and one from the Fifth.

They each handed over their reports.

The first which had been relayed across the river was from Schonberg. He had taken less than forty casualties and believed that casualties among the defenders were minimal. His two cohorts had stopped at the designated point except for the hundred and fifty who were galloping in to the ford to swing round behind the Seventh to be ready to move the towers forward if required. The rest were already infiltrating back to their start line.

The second report was from Claudius and simply stated that he would need another hour and a half to reduce the top of the wall to the required state. Crastus made a mental note to check the progress of that phase of the operation as soon as he re-ascended.

The third report, however, brought a grimace to his face as he found out that the right hand manoeuvre was taking considerable casualties, both to his own Fifth and also on the other bank to Schonberg's troops. It looked increasingly unlikely that any of the attackers would reach the river wall let along take part of it. Instinct told him to pull these men back, but he had to hold the defenders attention in that critical sector a while longer yet.

The morning was not yet half spent, but the tension had taken its toll already. He quickly drank and then relieved himself before clambering back into the basket. Leander was already there and the two relief signalmen joined them with alacrity as Crastus signed for the winch crews to earn their keep once more.

Once the basket had regained its operating height and the breathless winch crew had collectively headed for the water buckets, Crastus looked over at the walls of Dominique. Even with the naked eye he could see that the wall tops were rather more missing than intact. Mentally, he revised Claudius's cautious estimate and expected the operation there to be complete within the hour. These new tread wheel catapults were so much stronger and quicker than the simple trebuchets of his youth.

He was about to order the next phase to the attack when a recognizable peal of trumpet calls rang out from Claudine. It was the order to sally forth, Schonberg's fervent wish appeared to have been answered as a century sallied from the postern gate on Claudine's river wall and began to cover the ground towards his ditch and earthwork defences. Crastus could well imagine the delight on his subordinate commander's face as he watched this tempting morsel approach his seemingly weakened flank. They, of course, had no idea that so many men waited out of sight behind the earthworks.

Crastus swore as he realized the truth, such a small attacking force was being effectively sacrificed to establish if the move across the river was real or not. If Schonberg met the counter attack with overwhelming force, as per his orders, the defending commander would know that the move was a feint. Was Schonberg astute enough to realise this? Unable to influence the battle on the north bank, he could only watch the unfolding drama.

With such an experienced commander as Schonberg there was, of course, nothing to worry about. The highly visible sentries sounded the alarm and only a handful of soldiers appeared on the earthwork mound to join them. These were not simply the guards left behind as the defenders supposed; they were all sharpshooters to the man. They let fly and the attacking force melted away even before they reached the ditch. Schonberg later reported that only two men of the attacking unit even reached the bank of the ditch and the chastened survivors had turned and fled straight back to the safety of the walls. The plan remained intact.

"Signal Maximus Seven."

Within minutes, a new sound intruded on them as the catapults within AnnMarie began to open up. The large missiles thrown by these were not the rocks being thrown by the other catapults but instead threw black powder bombs. Crastus and Leander watched in interest as the clay pots containing the precious chemical arched high into the air and crashed down into the middle of Isabelle. Even before the first salvo of three pots had reached the high point of their trajectory, a burning ball of weighted straw followed them. Leander noted with approval that the catapult launching the fire bomb did so from a different section of AnnMarie. Obviously Cesca was being very careful about the handling routines for the precious but volatile chemical. At this distance, he could not hear the pots land and smash but only an instant after the burning ball of straw disappeared from sight behind the wall there was an echoing hollow boom and a large cloud of smoke billowed up. Obviously Cesca's new tactic was working.

Soon another volley flew through the air, followed by its separate fire bomb. Again they were rewarded with the sound of an explosion. This time the plume of smoke rose steadily after the initial explosion. Something flammable had been hit and this added to the defender's problems. Each following wave of projectiles was aimed at a slightly different point within the fortress. Occasionally, there was no explosion as the vagaries of wind and dynamics took the flaming projectile off course. On one occasion, there was an extra large explosion; obviously an earlier cluster had been set off by a subsequent one's flamer.

Crastus was not entirely happy with the idea of using so much of the precious powder for a diversionary purpose but felt that the effect would sway the enemy into assuming Isabelle was the target that the expenditure was worth it.

Checking on the progress of the bombardment of the wall on Dominique showed him that the top stonework was virtually gone. Indeed, Claudius's rate of fire appeared to have slackened off considerably as he readied his troops for the next phase of the attack.

"Signal Claudius Eight," said Crastus as he continued to drive the plan forwards.

"Signal Schonberg Ten and Maximus Ten," he added the agreed pull back signals to the twin attacks on the river forts on the other side of the battlefield. Although this was out of sequence, he knew all of his commanders would know why this was so.

Claudius's easternmost catapults now stopped firing and began to re-orientate themselves to attack Isabelle. Within ten minutes, they were hurling rocks over the wall to add to what was hopefully considerable carnage within. Their rate of fire stepped up and Crastus knew the crews were sweating profusely as their crew chiefs exhorted them to maximum effort.

Meanwhile, the relieved commanders on the other flank had pulled their troops back out of range of the murderous defensive fire they had been submitted too since fairly early on in the proceedings.

Now, it was time to crank up the pace and finish the job.

"Signal Maximus Nine and Schonberg Nine."

The rest of the Fighting Fifth rose from their positions and formed up in standard formation to attack across the face of AnnMarie and into the flank of Isabelle. Schonberg's diversionary forces were now approaching from the ford and were, as per the late modification to the plan, approaching the city from behind the assault towers. To increase the difficulty in the defender's accurately estimating their numbers, they milled around, demonstrating to be a force far larger than reality.

On cue, a series of trumpet calls pealed from the city wall and the main gate of Zampetta crashed open as another full cohort of the defenders pushed out. The causeway linking them to either Isabelle or Dominique passed obliquely in front of the walls of AnnMarie. Knowing that they would be running the gauntlet of fire from the captured fortress, the moving troops, identified by their pennants as the third cohort of the twelfth, formed up with their shields providing the old fashioned half-testudo to protect them from any arrows coming from AnnMarie. They, however, assumed that the majority of the Fifth inside the fort were already engaged in attacking the forts on either side.

Planning for this, Crastus had infiltrated another full cohort into the fort the previous night and they now lined up almost in target range fashion to savage their opponents. The testudo had been very successful when, hundreds of years earlier, the Roman army had fought mainly on foot. Now, most fighting was as cavalry or as mounted infantry and had necessitated a smaller size shield which reduced the overlap between the shields. The testudo was thus more vulnerable and the officers commanding the archers knew this well. As the men charged along the causeway, momentary gaps opened in the defensive shield wall as individual men adjusted position. With the weight of fire being directed their way, as often as not an arrow would find the gap and a man would fall wounded or dead. As he fell, this caused the gap to increase in size until it could be plugged. Sometimes, the fall of one man would cause the next to trip resulting in a larger gap still. Soon, the testudo was halfway across leaving a trail of bodies and broken groaning men behind them. As they approached the fork which would reveal which fortress they were heading for, Crastus held his breath.

The sheer discipline of these troops was something to be admired, enemy or not. They were true Roman legionaries. Crastus let his breath out explosively as they took the left fork, and proceeded exactly to where he wanted them to be. Having suffered such punishment, the unit would not be able to take part in any further movement today and as long as the plan was followed correctly, they would be trapped within the walls of Isabelle with their other comrades and effectively isolated and powerless for the rest of the campaign.

Finally, the gates closed behind the last of the unit and, by the look of the bodies and wounded strung out along the causeway, they must have suffered at least twenty to thirty percent casualties in the process.

Caught up in the action of the moment, no one had even noticed that the signal had not been sent for that part of the battle. The defender's own actions had triggered the response of its own accord. Crastus smiled and immediately ordered the final phase of the plan.

"Signal Claudius Twelve."

As soon as the signal had been acknowledged, he ordered the basket lowered and, on reaching ground level, signalled for his horse whilst Leander ascended again to keep a lookout for any unforeseen actions across the battlefield.

Crastus galloped nearer to the action the Storming Seventh left their siege lines and started towards the ragged topped wall of Dominique. Simultaneously, the small party from the Seventeenth stopped milling around and began harnessing their mounts to the running gear of the assault towers in preparation for turning them against the same fort.

Quickly, the assaulting troops charged into action running full tilt for the base of the wall. Meanwhile, in an addition to the plan arranged with Maximus over breakfast, the Fifth, standing as if to assault Isabelle, now closed the range and began to pepper the outer wall with arrow fire to further reduce supporting fire from there.

With everybody's attention elsewhere, the defenders did not notice Schonberg's small force surreptitiously crossing the ditch and the first the defenders of Claudine knew, about being under fire again was when the arrows came over. Although the number of archers was small, after all they were supposed to be on the other side of the river, the harassing fire was enough to draw a number of the defenders away from supporting Dominique.

It was by no means a foregone conclusion, but by the time Crastus had arrived at Claudius's forward command post, to find Claudius was leading the assault troops himself, the sheer speed and ferocity of the assault was carrying the wall. Crastus watched in amazement as the well-drilled troops flung ladders up against the wall, threw grapples up and literally flowed up. He caught his breath when he saw the familiar figure of Claudius halfway up one ladder but relaxed when he realized that the bright ceremonial armour had been discarded in favour of standard field kit which meant the opposition were less likely to pick him out. The construction of Dominique was slightly different from AnnMarie their first prize, as there were doors on the towers opening directly onto the wall itself. Given the need to defend against ship borne attack which would need men on the wall quicker, this was understandable on the riverside wall, but typical Roman need for order had in this case created a weakness. Claudius was no sooner on the wall top than he was leading a sizeable group of men straight for the door in the corner tower.

In what appeared to be a blink of an eye, but in reality was probably a couple of minutes, they had broken through the door and were inside the tower. Meanwhile, other troops cleared the top of the wall and began to fight their way down into the body of the fort. Suddenly, fighting broke out on the tower top and, within seconds, the flag of the Seventh appeared there. With the tower top gone, with the outer wall taken it would not be long before the defenders realised they were facing inevitable defeat. To shouts of *Traditum, Tradidi,* the men of the seventh exhorted their countrymen to lay down their arms.

Slowly, the sounds of fighting died away. Inside the main body of the fort, the defenders began to lay down their arms. The garrisons of the two inner towers took a little longer to persuade their officers that it was a lost cause, but they followed suit. The garrison of the inner river tower took a different approach. Suddenly, they burst out onto the river wall and jumped over the sides carrying inflated water skins. They hoped that the sluggish current would carry them down to the city. Sportingly, the men of the Seventh let them go. A flagman appeared on the wall and began signalling to the Sky Nest *Twelve done* to signal the capture of Dominique not realizing that Crastus was already nearby. Not long after, a tired and blood stained Claudius had the postern gate opened and walked back to his command post. As soon as he saw Crastus was waiting for him, he grinned and punched the air. The rest of his staff cheered.

The second of the Seven Sisters had fallen.

Chapter 15 - Claudine

That night, a jubilant staff gathered in Crastus's tent to celebrate their victory and discuss the plan for the next stage of the campaign.

"They say a plan never survives contact with the enemy, but that one certainly did!"

Everyone laughed at Leander's comment except Maximus and Crastus. Over four hundred men of the combined force would never put on armour again, either through their death or their wounds being so serious. The lightly wounded numbered nearly the same and some of those would not be fit for duty for several weeks. Claudius himself had suffered a cut on the arm which he maintained was minor, but probably was more serious. Nevertheless, the larger than life second-in-command eagerly discussed with Schonberg how to add the title 'Lion of Dominique' tastefully to his personal standard already encrusted with many such legends.

"I nearly shat myself when the commander of the Eastern tower responded to 'Lay down your sword' by opening the door to his tower and marching out to surrender. I was trying so hard not to laugh when the imbecile did exactly that and laid his sword at my feet. He was trembling," said Claudius as he regaled his fellow commander with the juicier bits of his own personal battle that afternoon.

Crastus was shrewd enough to let his subordinates let off steam for a while, but not for too long. When he felt they had shed enough exuberance and imbibed enough watered wine, he signalled Maximus and the *primus pilus* called them to order with.

In the ensuing silence, Crastus brought their minds back onto business.

"Today was very well done, gentlemen, but you have to remember that we cannot sustain this level of casualties simply reducing the outer forts. If we do, we will not have enough men left to take the city, even leaving Isabelle to wither on the vine. So the question, is do we stick with the original plan and attack Gabrielle in three days or do we try Schonberg's little trick against Claudine?"

Having watched several dozen members of the garrison of Dominique escape by floating downriver using inflated water skins to float on the current, Schonberg wanted to try a night attack on Claudine by a similar method.

"It has the advantage that the chosen men will approach the fortress silently and almost invisibly," Schonberg urged, seeking support for the idea.

Maximus took the devil's advocate position.

"Lacking armour and beyond support range of anybody other than the troops on the walls of Dominique, they will be easy prey if discovered. "

"Yes, but with the rest of two cohorts of the legion ready to act in support, I will be able to quickly take advantage of any breach in the defences. The risk is worth it – we could capture Claudine without the expense of a frontal assault. As Crastus just said, we can't afford to continue at the loss rate for the last three attacks."

The sly reference to the first failed attack on Dominique brought a frown to Claudius's face. So far, his legion had sustained the most casualties overall.

As it did not involve any preparation time in terms of heavy equipment, he was ready to go tomorrow night and this was the clinching argument that swung the majority of the staff his way.

The rest of the army could continue the preparations for assaulting Gabrielle and that assault could simply be delayed if Schonberg's attack was successful. If it wasn't, then the assault on Gabrielle could go ahead as planned. The siege equipment was not needed on the North bank, anyway. Isabelle was not going to be attacked, so there was every reason to move it anyway.

His mind made up, Crastus gave his subordinate the go-ahead and called the meeting to a close.

That night, it rained heavily for an hour or so which created several problems for the attackers. Firstly, the extra weight of the water soaking into the protective uncured hides on the siege equipment made them harder to move across what the now softer terrain. Similarly, the fall of rain in the hills some miles to the north had increased the flow of the current in the river making any attempt on Claudine dangerous in the extreme. Even the ford upstream was more dangerous and one galloper lost his horse and very nearly his own life trying it. As a result, both attacks were put back for twenty-four hours and the entire army on the southern side welcomed the respite. On the other bank, however, Schonberg's men, so little involved in the fighting to date were chomping at the bit.

The defenders position was becoming increasingly hopeless. With two of the forts lost and nearly half of their remaining combat power isolated at the end of a long thin causeway, easily in range of both AnnMarie and Dominique and thus effectively cut off, there were not enough troops to hold all of the lengths of wall they needed too. To meekly surrender any of the other forts was out of the question. If Claudine fell then the whole complex was open to attack from a completely naked flank. If Eloise was given up, then both Claudine and Beatrice were isolated, although Beatrice did connect to Gabrielle via the river wall. Gabrielle could not be given up as it housed the mechanisms for lowering the sluice gates and restoring the river to its natural level. Isabelle had been rendered impotent, anyway. The civilian population, never really fond of the Pretender, even less so now he was dead, was getting increasingly restless. They had no desire to see their homes and their city sacked. The trouble was, there was nowhere for them to run. This was the last major city held by the Pretender's army. Every other base once controlled had surrendered to Valerian's troops and were happily professing undying loyalty to him and his line.

Crastus and his staff had another night of uninterrupted sleep; their opponents did not have that luxury as small units of Crastus' men repeatedly made noisy demonstrations against each of the forts in turn. The commanders of the entrapped legions could do nothing but respond just in case.

The following evening, after a nice clear Italian autumn day, Schonberg reported earlier than usual that he was ready to attack that night. Sensing his subordinate's intentions, he issued a direct order that Schonberg was not himself to take part in the water borne part of the operation. The crestfallen look on the big German's face told Crastus that his intuition had been right; Schonberg had fully intended to lead the attack himself. Crastus detailed Leander to accompany Schonberg that night as a way of ensuring that his impetuous friend did not disobey the order and take the risk anyway.

That evening, a small group of the Seventeenth's eighth cohort, dressed in tunics quickly dyed a mottled black and brown armed only with short swords and daggers wrapped in oiled cloth. Clutching inflated water skins, they waded into the river several hundred yards above the fort. The bend in the river hid their activity from the fortress and the nearly moonless night provided excellent cover. The current had returned to its normal sluggish state and the men were able to ease themselves about a third of the way out and control their position noiselessly as they drifted towards their target.

Several minutes passed and keen eyed observers on the river bank noted their passing as they reached and then passed the entrance to the ditch. A runner was quickly dispatched whilst the assault troops poised for action behind the earthwork readied themselves for action. Last minute preparations were almost silent and the sentries on the walls of Claudine remained oblivious. The plank bridges were slid ever closer to the top of the earthwork, the men always careful not to silhouette themselves against the sky.

A second runner appeared; the water borne team had reached the corner of the fort and were angling in towards the wall there. Still, no alarm sounded. The men reached the bottom of the wall and cut slits in the water bags so that they would sink, then began to uncoil the ropes they carried. Quickly, the lead men on each climbing team began to shim up the wall, paying the ropes out behind them. Reaching the top, they realized that, in the defenders utter folly, there were no sentries on the riverside wall. Tying the ropes around the buttresses, they signalled for the other troops to climb up and dashed into the shadows in an attempt to avoid detection. A small team of three men swung another rope over the inside of the wall, swung down and crept up on the postern gate guard. The struggle that ensued was almost noiseless but not quite quiet enough. One sentry on the adjoining wall heard a noise and issued a challenge.

That challenge was loud enough to echo out to the rest of the Seventeenth poised to attack. Like a coiled spring suddenly released, they leapt into action. Before the startled sentries could raise a full alarm, the men had run the bridges across the ditch and were sprinting for the walls. The original challenge was now forgotten about as the direct attack gathered momentum. Unnoticed by the defenders in the darkness and confusion, the *primus pilus* and his first century of the first cohort of the seventeenth angled their attack towards the corner. They arrived at the postern gate without being spotted and, with their own men controlling the defences of the gate, lost no time in entering. Soon, madness and confusion reigned inside as these, the most experienced troops in the legion, fanned out in all directions in small groups to attack specific targets.

The tribune in charge of the fort had only half-climbed into his armour in his quarters and was still trying to shake off the vestiges of sleep when his dying guard toppled backwards through the doorway, the body followed by the men who had killed him. Unable to defend himself properly and unwilling to surrender, he died very quickly.

Other parties of the invading troops fanned out over the interior of the fort and several sections of the defenders were bottled up inside their own barracks by strategically placed archers firing through the doorway from the darkness into the torch lit rooms. On the outer wall, things quickly became desperate, too. With their reinforcement troops unable to get to them and with three centuries attacking them, the sentries on the wall were quickly overwhelmed and the Seventeenth was soon in control of the fort except the towers.

Again, as with Dominique, the walls had doorways into the towers and one by one these were assaulted, taken and the towers captured. Within one hour of the first alarm, the fortress was theirs.

Schonberg now had his own triumph to match Crastus' and Claudius's; this time with far fewer casualties. Another of the Seven Sisters had fallen.

Chapter 16 - River

With a definite sense of déjà vu, Crastus smiled as he watched his staff. With the current rate of progress, it was becoming almost natural that the evening staff meeting was as much of a celebration as a serious planning session. Nevertheless, it would be impossible under the circumstances to deny the irrepressible German his right to celebrate his off the wall victory. The capture of Claudine had cost a mere fifteen dead and only twenty-three wounded, most only lightly. The Claudine garrison had been so taken by surprise by that no effective opposition had been mounted.

Having had an earlier conversation with his chief interrogator, he had more news for his commanders that they certainly did not suspect. It was time to spring his surprises on them.

"Your attentions please, gentlemen. I think I have news for you that will improve your mood even further. Claudius, do you remember the young Tribune who surrendered to you two days ago?"

"How could I forget? As he approached me he actually clanked – his armour was several sizes too big. When he stood up after laying his sword at my feet he was trembling so much he actually rattled!"

Claudius was beside himself at the memory and bent over laughing, holding his sides.

"Do you remember the name he gave you?"

"Gods, yes! That was the best bit the young whippersnapper gave his name as Scipio Africanus. I mean as if he could trace his ancestry back a thousand years to the hero of the war on Carthage,"

The rest of the staff was laughing as well now, except for Maximus whose face showed the dawning of comprehension as to where this was going.

"Claudius, his armour. It didn't fit properly you say? Was it silver with an embossed griffin's head on the breastplate?"

"Yes. It was far too good for such a young puppy to adorn himself with."

Crastus intervened before Maximus could blurt it out.

"Claudius, that was no ordinary Tribune you captured. Some fifteen years ago, a Legate most of us know, spent a winter with Maximus and I in the snowy passes in the mountains in Transalpine Gaul and regaled us with the story of how his family was descended from the heroes of the Second Punic War. Not only did he claim direct lineage from Scipio, but also from his patron, Cato. That Legate went on to higher office, and aimed for the highest office of all until we forced him to fall on his own sword at Salerno."

The dawning of realisation on the faces of the rest of the officers was priceless.

"That's right, gentlemen. Claudius didn't capture merely a Tribune but none other than Scipio, the youngest son of the Pretender, Galerius!"

Claudius's smile came even broader as he realized the import of his capture and the probable reward from his emperor. Then he grimaced as he realized what the young man's fate would be at the hands of Valerian.

Crastus, however, watched Schonberg intently. The big blond German was obviously pondering something and they could see on that guileless face the moment he reached a conclusion.

"Claudius, just describe that armour to me again."

Before Claudius could replay Crastus interrupted.

"That's right, his older brother was a senior tribune in the Twelfth, and he had been posted to command the garrison you destroyed last night. Your *primus pilus* ran his sword through the eldest son of the Pretender."

He continued. "Now we know why they were prepared to stand and fight here. They were protecting the last two surviving male heirs to the Pretender's claim to the throne. There had been rumours that the youngest had been enlisted into the Twelfth just before Salerno, but there had been no hard facts. The Twelfth saw very little action that day, as you know, and withdrew across the mountains in good order. Two cohorts of the Ninth managed to catch and rout their rearguard, but that was all. Now we know why they did not join in the main battle. Their last orders must have been to defend the boys. The elder one had been through basic training but the lad we captured had been too young before the war started; that's why he folded so easily. He had no military staff training whatsoever. He was a boy caught up in a man's war. The commander of the Twelfth should have kept them close to himself rather than trying to let them perform as Tribunes in the forts. He must be crucially short of experienced officers to allow that to happen."

He paused, "Now what does that tell us about the enemy? More importantly, what can we do to exploit that?"

Crastus allowed the news he had delivered to sink in and the weight of the questions give his staff pause to ponder.

When he felt that the mood of the meeting had returned to the sober if not sombre level he required, he continued.

"Having taken three of the forts on the Southern or Eastern side, they have to expect us to continue assaulting the fortresses from the outside one by one. Logically, we should attack Eloise or Gabrielle next; bearing in mind they don't know we won't be attacking Isabelle. If we follow this course of action, and our original plan was of course to attack Gabrielle next, we will keep our siege lines short and will not present them with any weak points to exploit. If we go for Beatrice next, or even the city itself, our perimeter will be extended and stretched. Bear in mind, they have the best part of four thousand men pocketed in Isabelle now, so we have to keep a substantial force ready to defend against any counter attack from there."

Each of the men present pondered the questions posed by Crastus and during the silence he took the opportunity to send a messenger to fetch Gaius "The Rat" as he already knew that his intelligence chief would be able to enlighten them further.

Nobody was prepared to advance more than a semblance of an answer to the weighty questions posed by Crastus and the arrival of Gaius a couple of minutes later was very welcome as a result. Gaius would normally attend these staff meetings but the fall of two of the Sisters in such quick succession had meant there had been too many prisoners to process and not a few civilians whose loyalty needed to be assessed. Indeed, he and his staff had uncovered several legionnaires and even a centurion posing as civilians in an attempt to escape capture. On Crastus' orders, they had been whisked away to the prison camp to be reprocessed as recruits. After all, initiative was not something he wanted to suppress.

The interrogation of those prisoners had revealed many things to the expert questioner and he had been getting ready for the summons since his earlier meeting with Crastus that afternoon.

"Gaius, if you would, please, tell us what you have learned about the enemy dispositions and command structure."

Crastus leaned back and relaxed for the bulk of Gaius's report since he had already received it earlier but now wanted to observe the reactions of his senior staff.

"Let's start with what we know." Gaius picked up the pointer and moved over to the sand table. He pointed to each fortress in turn. "AnnMarie is ours; Isabelle contains four cohorts of the Twelfth legion, commanded by their *pilus primus* and two tribunes. They are bottled in and going nowhere, any attempt to break out back to the city will cost them too dearly. The mood within the Twelfth is sombre and morale low. I'll tell you why shortly. Dominique and Claudine are in our hands. Eliane was expected to be our next target, so the bulk of the forces on the northern shore are enclosed there. There are three cohorts of the Fourteenth inside the place and only one and a half inside Beatrice."

He paused to let this sink in.

"Gabrielle is held by the remaining two cohorts of the Twelfth, including their replacements. As the river forts are the strongest, they have put as few troops in place as they dare to retain the balance of the Fourteenth and the Eleventh as reserves and also garrison for the city.

"The enemy dispositions we were given earlier were in part a ruse to cover the presence of the two princes, and also to try to trick us into attacking the wrong point – any of the three strongest, Gabrielle, Isabelle or Eloise.

"As we already know, the commander of the Eleventh, Agrippa, died in our assault on AnnMarie. What we now know is that command of the Twelfth has devolved to the legate, Flavius, after his uncle, Lanatus, was badly wounded in a skirmish the day before Salerno and is not with his command."

There was a collective gasp around the room at this morsel of news. Lanatus was as revered a legion commander as Crastus himself. To find that the most capable leader the enemy had left was not even present was good news indeed. There was more to follow.

"Flavius allowed the two young princes to sway his judgment and gave them the commands and attachments they wanted and due to the current incapacity of Sergius the commander of the Fourteenth because of his gout, young Flavius is in de facto command of the entire defences.

"The wall of Eliane facing the river," he tapped the relevant section of the model as he spoke, "is suffering from a serious internal collapse and as a result will not take the weight of any sizeable force in its defence. It certainly cannot take the stress of any catapults being mounted there, and there are apparently concerns about the two towers on that side too. The river route into the city is therefore safe from major flanking fire."

Again he paused, the pointer trailing in the groove in the sand box which represented the river.

"The city itself is in turmoil. No man in uniform will venture outside of the barracks without armour and then only in groups of four or more. There have been a number of ugly incidents and the reprisals taken have inflamed things further. There is no way the civilian population wants to face the prospect of our army sacking the city."

Crastus leant forward and asked the question uppermost in everyone's mind.

"So, gentlemen, do we attack Gabrielle or do we use the river to attack the city?"

With the heavy equipment already in position, Maximus was the advocate for attacking the river fort at the other end of the complex, Gabrielle. With one fortress taken by each legion, he was just as concerned about retaining the primacy of his own Fighting Fifth as the true strategic imperative. He flushed when Crastus looked at him reproachfully. Schonberg, still energized with the success of taking Claudine at such little cost, was all for the waterborne attack. Claudius was the swing vote. His Seventh legion had taken more casualties than either of the others and he still needed time to complete the personnel transfer and meld the replacements into his battle-hardened front line units.

The heated discussion between the staff went on long into the night. Some favoured the original plan of reducing the fortresses one by one, opening the sluice gates and draining the land before finally assaulting the city from three sides. Others espoused the more daring approach, with the western river end secured and the news about the weakness at Eliane, they wanted to use the boats and rafts and attack the city from the river.

The river attack had a lot going for it as the city walls on the river side were pierced by many gateways leading to the wharves. Defensively, that side was a nightmare and the whole purpose of the ring of fortresses was to prevent any such attack. Once the city fell, the defenders would be isolated into effectively three pockets, only Beatrice and Gabrielle were able to cover each other, and they could be mopped up individually. The big problem was that the siege lines would be stretched to the limit making the army vulnerable to counter-attack.

Crastus was now faced with the decision. He had already weighed up the two sides to the argument but had wanted his staff to arrive at a consensus by themselves if possible. The glory hounds, including both Schonberg and eventually Claudius, were all for abandoning the planned strategy and attacking up the river. Most of the rest were for the more conservative original plan which was to attack Gabrielle next. Crastus was surprised to see Maximus; *primus pilus* was almost always given to a conservative leader, finally changing sides and siding with the more adventurous group. As a result, he listened most attentively to the senior centurion's ideas he was advancing.

This was the final straw that confirmed his own decision. With the rest of the staff beginning to see the sense of Maximus' arguments, the consensus had formed. They would attack from the river because the opportunity so presented was not simply just a way of ending the siege quickly, but also was potentially a way of doing so without suffering the casualty numbers experienced in the two assaults on Dominique.

Hs mind made up, he stopped the discussion in mid-flow and announced his final plan. It would be the river and it would be in three days with the Seventeenth leading the way.

Chapter 17 - City

The morning, three days after the decision had been taken, was as bright and sunny as was expected for this time of year. The intervening three days had gone very much according to plan. The troops in the remaining fortresses had remained bottled up and had made no attempt to break out or move between them. The troops in the city had not launched any counterattacks or any attempts to reinforce the fortresses via the vulnerable causeway system.

The short causeway between the city and Gabrielle was beyond arrow range and several couriers galloped back and forth along it on each day. The river wall over the sluice gates enabled messengers to pass to Beatrice, too, so these three parts of the complex were at least in communication with each other. The troops in Eloise and Isabelle were isolated and could only communicate by flag signals. Those signals could, of course, be read by Crastus's troops in the forts he held, and the military codes in use were the same for both sides.

Crastus would have set up contingency plans for this eventuality, and he was sure that Lanatus or Agrippa would have done so as well. With them out of the picture, the command structure inside the city appeared too inexperienced and thus impotent to deal with their reality.

With two successful night attacks under their belt, several of the junior officers had expected the city assault to take place at night, too. Their seniors knew better. A large, coordinated, water borne attack would be too difficult to organise and control. The leaders inside the city had been deprived of the senior commanders with that kind of experience. As a result, the number of sentries on each wall had been doubled and the routine patrolling by larger groups had stepped up in frequency, too. Crastus's force was well rested after three days of relative inactivity. In contrast, the defenders were close to the edge having been kept awake and alert by the continuous series of small scale deceptive attacks by the attacking force for almost the entire seventy-two hours preceding the attack.

It never ceased to amaze Crastus just how these tactics continued to succeed. In the reverse situation, he would have either abandoned the complex already or have sallied in force against one part of the lines. He would especially have been ready to ambush such a deception and crush it with overwhelming force. This would have discouraged any further such movement. The defenders failed to do any of this and instead sat tight. As long as they continued to cooperate with him, he was quite happy.

Although the bend in the river concealed the flotilla of rafts from direct observation by the city, the construction of them had been observed and reported on by the occupants of Isabelle who had signalled their observations across to the city wall. However, with the siege engines massed opposite Gabrielle, it was difficult for Flavius and his officers to decide which direction the real attack was coming from. The previous day, several hundred feet of high woven screen had been erected along the river bank as if to shield the rafts from view by troops in Isabelle. This morning, the driver of a small cart carrying suppliers to be winched up the wall into

Dominique had apparently lost control and crashed through the screens. The centurion in charge had bellowed at the hapless man for ages in full view of the observers on Isabelle and the gaps in the screens had not been mended. The rafts remained empty. This information was quickly relayed back to the City from Isabelle.

Meanwhile, the catapults were aiming their projectiles into Gabrielle and the rate of fire picked up. The two huge assault towers were doused with water and rolled into start positions and the Fifth moved into position as if to assault. As the catapult rate of fire picked up and the massed troops edged to just outside arrow range, with no activity on the river, Flavius had to act. The city gate crashed open and three centuries of the Fourteenth doubled across the short causeway into Gabrielle. As the gates boomed shut again the *Execute* signal was telegraphed from the Sky Nest. The signals did not need to be as complex as before since all of the parts of the plan were designed to occur simultaneously.

Yet again, Flavius had been lured into making the wrong decision and reinforcing the wrong part of his defences.

The catapults increased the range of their projectiles and now all of them were aiming for the area just inside the gatehouse connecting Gabrielle to the city. Now, the explosive bombs were added to the range of projectiles being fired and it quickly became apparent to the defenders that there was no real chance of leaving for the city. The use of unlit fuses on the black powder bombs followed up by incendiaries was this time less successful than when attacking Isabelle as the relatively long range made the aiming more difficult. The defending troops as well had also liberally doused the interior of the fort with water, lessening the effect.

Over on the other flank, the screens so deliberately wrecked were repaired by the sections hidden from view precisely for that purpose. The apparent hapless driver was actually the champion chariot driver for that legion and the centurion who had so loudly berated him was none other than his own brother. Deception and sleight of hand, yet again. Within seconds, the screens were again complete and behind them, the troops who had lain silently in wait behind a line of low earthworks on the bank swarmed forwards onto their assigned rafts.

Roman legions practiced water borne assaults against fortified targets infrequently. In this case, though, the Seventeenth had performed several such operations in previous years to reduce small garrisons of the Pretender's forces and were naturally the main component of the first wave. With practiced ease, the men shook themselves out into a double section, sixteen men, onto each raft and with one manning the steering oar at the back and one navigating from the front, the rest paddling they assembled at the left side of the river. The screens prevented observation from Isabelle and, by keeping to the left side of the river the walls of Claudine screened, from Eliane.

The leading rafts backed water for a few minutes to maintain station whilst the rest of the men boarded. As soon as the whole assault wave was ready, the signal was given and the men began to row slowly and silently down the river. When they had covered about a quarter of the distance to the city wharves, they came within sight of the city itself. With the cries of alarm echoing from the city, all vestige of stealth vanished and, as one, the occupants of the rafts began to paddle furiously towards their targets.

They quickly entered the 'friendly' canyon between the walls of Claudine and Dominique. Here, they were sheltered from any enemy fire but as soon as they exited the other side, this was no longer the case. The short space of time required to transit this point had been enough time for the commander of the garrison of Eliane to react. His troops lined the western wall and began to pour deadly arrow fire at the rafts. Thankfully, the information relating to the southern, river facing wall was accurate because the number of men manning this section was very low. Covering fire from Claudine was partially effective but, on board the rafts, men fell, some of them riddled by several arrows. They could hear the centurions on the wall roaring their men on and at the same time bellowing to pick their targets.

Not all of the archers in the fortress could stand on the wall and fire directly down onto the rafts. Several centuries had been drawn up in the courtyard in the middle and now their indirect plunging fire was added to the gauntlet. The men manning the walls of Claudine lay down as heavy a counter fire as they could. The garrison there, though, had been reduced to the minimum in order to provide the maximum force level possible for the assault. Men within Eloise fell, but not many and not quickly. This stretch of the river was the danger point of the entire gauntlet.

One raft lost all the oarsmen on the left side to the hail of arrows. The raft spun sideways under the impetus of the rowers on the other side and rammed into the rear of the raft just to the shoreward side of it. With both the steering oar and a couple of the rear oars gone, the two meshed together, drifting helplessly into the way of others. Confusion reigned in the middle of the river for a short period, but already the lead rafts were abreast of the downstream section of the city.

The bulk of the city garrison and the entire reaction force, tricked into believing they were going to be needed to help defend Gabrielle were completely out of position. Now, they raced across the city to join their heavily outnumbered comrades facing the full might of Schonberg's legion.

As soon as the leading raft reached a position opposite its designated landing point, a trumpet sounded and the rafts turned and rowed across the current, heading for land. The river behind them was littered with at least a dozen damaged or incapacitated rafts, most covered with dead and wounded men.

The catapults, previously attacking the gatehouse section of Gabrielle, now switched their aim in response to another signal from the Sky Nest and increased their range to its absolute maximum. Although winding the catapults now took twice as long, they could now reach the south eastern corner of the city from where they were sited. They were throwing incendiaries and quite quickly several small fires had started.

Contradictory orders were now issued and some of the men, rushing across the city to meet the attack on the wharves were turned around and sent back to help - or force, the civilians to put out the fires. Confusion reigned inside the city.

The first wave of rafts slammed into the wharves and immediately the soldiers on board leapt into action. With practiced ease, they sprinted along the wharves and made short work of the sentries encountered. For a brief moment, they were no longer under fire. As the first wave stormed along the wharves towards the river wall, the second wave of rafts shot through the canyon between Claudine and Dominique. The men on the other side of the river within Eloise now had to turn their attention to this second wave of rafts running the gauntlet.

The centurion in charge of the men on Wharf Three could not believe his luck. The sentries placed on the wharf itself had thrown down their weapons. Not only had the sentries asked for and been given quarter, but they had left the gate open. The sentries on the wall immediately above the gate, seeing they didn't have the numbers to prevent the capture of the gate, retreated along the wall. Shouting with triumph, his century stormed through and took up defensive positions to protect this valuable entry point.

The antiquated design of the defences had let the defenders down again. The ten foot wide stone platform that ran the length of the wall on the outside was brilliant for moving goods between ships or loading and unloading. It was, unfortunately, also brilliant for attacking troops to deploy rapidly to back up penetrations. Seeing this, the men on Wharf Two angled in to join their compatriots and before the defenders were able to react in sufficient force their moment had been lost. With sufficient force on the river wall and the wisdom to shut and bar all of the gates, they could have prevented incursion into the city itself. Now, the moment had passed.

None of the other teams had been so lucky, but with the flagman at the end of Wharf Three signalling ‘Breach’ the majority of the second wave responded and landed there or on the adjacent wharves. Five minutes later, a full cohort was braced for a counter attack and the third wave was running the gauntlet.

If the city troops had been in position from the start, things might have gone differently. . By the time Crastus and Schonberg landed with the fourth wave, there was no chance left to counterattack. By now, five further gates had been captured and fully a third of the river wall was in their hands. The fire from Eliane slackened off as the defenders stocks of arrows dwindled and their casualties mounted from the accurate suppressing fire from Claudine. The fifth wave suffered only minor casualties and landed virtually intact. Inside the city, the pandemonium caused by the brief incendiary bombardment in the northeast section together with the successful invasion of the riverside quarter had doubled and redoubled. Although they had thrown a cordon around the invading troops, reinforcements were forced to push their way through milling crowds of increasingly hysterical civilians, most of whom had no love for the defending troops.

Crastus’s forces were inside the city and in sufficient force to stay.

Chapter 18 - Withdraw

The situation facing Flavius as he fought to gain control of his own forces was nothing short of a nightmare. His enemy, despite longer lines of communication, were able to react to his every move. Twice he had pulled troops away from the north eastern corner only for the incendiary bombardment to start up again. Each time, the men had had to race back to deal with the fires. Schonberg's troops within the city probed cautiously forwards and whenever they found a weakness gobbled up another small part of the city. Sometimes just a house, sometimes as much as a street would change hands. One cohort in the far western river tower area was likely to be cut off if they didn't retreat , but if they did it would give Crastus almost a quarter of the city.

Faced with a commander's worst nightmare, he was unable to make decisions that were militarily sensible and positive. Nothing he now did stood any chance of success. The city was lost, he could only bow to the inevitable.

Ordering his nearly trapped Third cohort to retreat along the city wall in as good order as possible, he began to prepare to evacuate the rest of his troops into the river forts and make a last stand there. He was issuing orders in preparation for both this and the destruction of the palace when news of disaster struck.

The Tribune in charge of the Third cohort had obeyed his instructions to the letter. The men had formed up and marched along the city wall towards Gabrielle in full view of the astonished men of the Fighting Fifth manning the walls of AnnMarie Moaning about having been out of the fight for so long, they could not believe the scope of the target laid out before them. AnnMarie was the closest fort from the city and the troops marching along the city wall were well within accurate bow-shot range. Flavius had intended them to use the cover available but, not for the first time, the lack of experience of the junior officers showed. Suddenly, the marching troops were sprayed with an accurate and deadly arrow storm from the outer fort. Flavius could only watch in horror from his vantage point on the hill in front of the palace as more and more men fell. Not before time, one of the centurions shouted for his men to break ranks and they sprinted pell-mell for the staircases down into the city and out of the line of fire. Given Flavius's frame of mind at this point, it was lucky for the Tribune that he had been one of the first to fall.

Realizing all his options were gone, Flavius gave the command for the trumpet calls to sound the retreat.

The withdrawal order was heard by the vast majority of his men, but by now not all of them could obey. Many were trapped and surrounded in small pockets and were geared up to fight to the end.

Schonberg's men heard the signal, too, and redoubled their efforts to cut the opposing forces into smaller and smaller pockets and remove the chance to retreat.

The withdrawal order gave most of them an out and, one at a time, these small units began to surrender. Other units were so heavily engaged, that an attempt to withdraw would have been suicide so continued fighting even as their comrades on both flanks left them to their fate. Eventually, too, the survivors of these units realized the futility of their actions and threw down their weapons.

With holes opening up in the lines facing them, Schonberg's men raced forward to fill the void. Many were motivated by the opportunity to plunder, but most were after the glory of reaching the palace first. Each successive tier of the city fell the same way. Most of the cornered troops were allowed to surrender. Small pockets sometimes preferred to fight on and, occasionally, some of the separated units were overwhelmed by a sudden attack from the side or rear by the enraged civilians. Here, the fighting was at its bloodiest. No quarter was asked or given and the better armed legionnaires usually took several of the more lightly armed citizens with each of them.

The sheer confusion of the fight within the city was beyond the control of either general. The pall of smoke drifting down from the smouldering fires in the north eastern corner added to the general confusion. With the withdrawal order given, Flavius could no longer affect the outcome of the battle.

Flavius knew as he watched the horror unfold that within the city, his army was beaten. He turned to give the order to put the torches to the fabrics within the palace to at least deny its capture to Crastus, but the troops of the Seventeenth were already within the compound. He drew his own weapon, ready to fight to the end, knowing that capture was a far worse fate given Valerian's inventive cruelty.

A chance sling stone knocked his helmet askew and dazed him. Unable to function properly, he vaguely felt two of his aides gather him up and lead him off in the direction of Gabrielle and safety whilst the remainder of his staff prepared to sell their lives dearly to buy time for them to escape.

Crastus and Schonberg had impressed in emphatic terms that not only was widespread looting forbidden but any troops that could surrender or withdraw were to be allowed to do so. Flavius's gallant rearguard was therefore somewhat surprised when the attack on them was not pressed home and they were allowed to follow their commander in retreat.

Crastus had one final trick up his sleeve for the troops leaving the city via the causeway. With the troops from both sides intermingled, the catapult crews could no longer fire at the city without risking casualties to their own side. As a result, their aiming points had been shifted back to Gabrielle. At the far end of the causeway, the gatehouse was back under fire from the catapults outside its southern wall. The battered survivors of the city garrison had one further gauntlet to survive before getting to safety.

Chapter 19 - Palace

It was early evening before the city could be considered under control. Some small pockets of resistance still held out, but they were eliminated one by one. The only ones that would be more troublesome were the areas immediately around the towers at the corners facing Beatrice and Gabrielle and the main gatehouse itself. Crastus was confident that the men he had left in charge of those sectors were more than capable of dealing with them while keeping casualties to a minimum.

The civilian population of the city was another story. Loyalist almost to a man, they had never been happy under the Protector's rule. Like civilians everywhere, they had a sizable merchant class that, sniffing profit, had done a great deal of business with the occupiers. Crastus did not particularly blame them; it was the only way they had to put food on the table for their families, after all. Some of the civilian population thought otherwise, though, and already a number of brutal beatings and a few murders had been reported as vigilantes sought retribution for both real and imagined collaboration.

Crastus found himself in a quandary. Until he could bring more troops inside in safety, he had few enough troops to hold the city walls let alone provide a police force to keep the citizens from each other's throats.

In the end, he summoned the city council or at least the surviving members of that body that could be found to the palace compound at sundown. There were supposed to be eleven magistrates making up the city council. By one hour past sundown, they had only managed to locate six of them and bring them to the palace grounds. Two were known to have died at the hands of the mob, one was recovering from the burns he had received in fighting fires earlier in the day and could not be moved. The final two were assumed to be in hiding. This left Crastus with a dilemma; by Roman law he could reinstitute civil rather than martial law only if he could get a majority of the magistrates to agree. Given the natures of the six men in front of him, he didn't think that they could agree that water was wet!

"Roman citizens. Listen to me."

Like a flock of hens disturbed by the presence of a fox, they still did not quiet down. He tried again, louder this time.

"Romans! Listen to me!"

Still, he could not get their attention. Shaking his head, he nodded to the *primus pilus* of the Seventeenth, loaned to him by Schonberg for this meeting. His parade ground bellow shattered the hubbub and silence ensued. Crastus was able to proceed with a more normal tone of voice.

"Gentlemen, thank you. I am going to ask you a simple question and please think very carefully about your answer. Your livelihood and possibly even your lives depend on your response."

He paused to allow the tension to build.

"I can either return government of the populace of this city to the control of the magistrates or I can retain martial law. You, gentlemen, must decide. You may very well feel personally safer with my men patrolling the streets, but let me tell you that is a chimera. I do not have enough troops to both patrol this city effectively and to garrison the walls as well. In order to meet the Emperor's wishes, I must reduce the other fortresses within days. If I cannot use my men for this purpose, the military law I will enforce will be of the highest severity. Order will be restored and all breaches of it will be dealt with summarily. That will include anybody that I or my officers deem to be inciting trouble.

"If I take my troops off the walls, there is a high probability that a counter attack could carry at least part of the city. With the current disposition of forces and the casualties already incurred, my lines are stretched outside the city and, as such, I cannot weaken them substantially to reinforce the city.

"Make your decision, but do it quickly."

He turned on his heel and left them to reach their own decision. He hoped it would not take too long. Schonberg, watching quietly from the side, winked as he passed.

"I'll wager they'll give you the decision you want within the hour. How about a barrel of that northern ale you are partial too?"

Crastus smiled back and they touched palms to confirm the wager. His last point was of course not quite true. If the trapped besieged defenders in any of the forts broke out, he would be able to prevent them linking up with each other to present him with any real problems and would, quite happily, let them melt into the countryside where they would do him no harm.

That night he fully intended to bring in another cohort of the Fifth to bolster the garrison but would still prefer to allow the council to police the city itself.

Schonberg did not win his bet. The arguments ran on long into the night but finally Crastus extracted the required consensus from them, and signing the necessary documents, handed policing over to the civilian authorities saving only that military personnel were only subject to military discipline.

Several hours later than planned, he was finally able to grab something to eat and deal with anything urgent relating to the immediate defences. With Claudius, Maximus and several other staff members still outside the complex, the normal staff meeting had to be forgone.

Early the following morning, having assured themselves that the city was indeed quiet and that the troops in the surrounded forts seemed perfectly willing not to venture out, dressed in plain armour Crastus and Schonberg slipped back out of the city so that they could confer with their colleagues.

Arriving at Claudius's near palatial command tent, they breakfasted heartily and discussed with him the direction the next step should take.

The decision to leave Isabelle alone and let the troops within stew impotently was a given in the discussion. Elaine on the north bank was able to harass troop movements in and out of the city proper but had terrain against them in terms of being able to attack any of the emplacements already taken. There was only one narrow front open to attack the fortress from the outside. It was also, like Isabelle heavily garrisoned.

The paired fortresses of Gabrielle and Beatrice were the tough nut that had to be cracked. Each could give the other covering fire, and it was also where the staff of the Twelfth and Fourteenth were based. Although they had not distinguished themselves in this campaign so far didn't mean they couldn't. Once they fell, it was believed that offers of clemency would enable both the other forts to surrender without much more bloodshed.

The wall that connected the two fortresses over the top of the sluice gates that dammed the river was actually hollow freely allowing the passage of men unseen between the two. In an attack, like the previous feints, was mounted only against one of the pair, troops could be moved to the point of attack. The only way to prevent this was to attack both simultaneously and Crastus didn't have enough men to do this without weakening his other forces to the point that the siege could be broken.

The three commanders now had to decide how to solve this conundrum.

Chapter 20 - Rome

Valerian paused half way through reading the reports he had received that morning from Crastus. He had already read the report sent by Claudius through different and secret channels. Claudius was certain that Crastus did not suspect that he was also under orders to report directly to Valerian. Valerian gave his army commander more respect than that and was equally sure that Crastus would be aware of if not actually intercepting and copying those reports himself.

With three of the fortresses in the army's control and having captured the city more or less intact, they were getting close to completing the task he had set them.

It looked very likely that he would be able to fulfil his vow to celebrate the solstice there. Now, he had to make a decision as the subtle politics of the situation came into play. Valerian was not particularly popular with the patrician class or aristocracy of the city and, unlike the fourth and fifth centuries, Rome was the centre of power. The mob and the common people and, above all, the army had been his up until he had pushed Galerius into open rebellion. The provinces remained loyal, but he had to be careful around the Senate.

A waiting messenger was sent scurrying to fetch Gaius. Alone of his advisers, the chamberlain was savvy enough to help reach the correct decision.

When Gaius arrived, he did not give the man chance to perform the rituals of entering the emperor's presence.

"Well, what do you think of the situation at Zampetta now?"

Gaius, caught in the middle of the act of genuflection, regained his feet as gracefully as possible and perched on the couch Valerian gestured impatiently towards.

"Well, sire, I am sure that the capture of the city, effectively intact, and with a working civil government is something that gives cause for celebration."

"No! I don't want platitudes! I can get them from anyone in court, I want your opinions."

Gaius had seen this mood many times before; he had anticipated the summons from the emperor and was ready with an answer which was a question of its own.

"Sire, it depends entirely on what you perceive to be the biggest benefit to you. If you announce the victory so far, then you can accrue the credit for that. Your pilgrimage to the palace and temple at Zampetta can be planned. This way, you take the major portion of the credit for the final victory.

"If you then hamper Crastus by withdrawing part of his force or restricting his supply, you can make any subsequent defeat his and his alone. However, if he succeeds under those conditions, his image will be boosted whilst your foresight will be commended. He wouldn't have needed as many troops as he asked for. On the other hand, if you are seen to actively send him support and possibly reinforcements and he fails, his reputation is sunk without a trace. If he wins, then the glory is still yours.

"Another possibility is to say nothing publicly, reduce his effectiveness by reducing or delaying his supplies and privately inform him he has less time than he thinks to achieve total victory.

"Finally, the damage sustained to the walls of Dominique, the breach in the wall of AnnMarie and the damage to the city's commercial districts could be used as a pretext for his removal from command. Similarly, the recognition of the city magistrates despite their obvious collaboration with the Pretender could be used as a suitable pretext."

Valerian pondered the options laid in front of him, but continued to watch Gaius like a hawk. He felt that the devious chamberlain had another idea or two up his sleeve. Sensing the emperor's steely glaze, Gaius let the silence build the tension he wanted. Within the palace, it was always wheels within wheels within wheels.

"Of course, there is another option . . ."

Valerian rose to the bait like a snapper.

"Go on"

"If you were to undertake a more complex plan . . ."

"Just get on with it!"

"Well, let's say we tell Crastus he has a month less to complete the capture as you now need to visit the temple earlier for some reason. We delay his supply convoys by a few days as well. His position will become much more complicated. At the same time, you censure him for the damage to the fortress walls and insist that he reinstates martial law in the city because you want the magistrates put to the question."

"I see where this leads. But what possible pretext can I give to bring the pilgrimage forwards. After all, there are no major festivals or religious days before midsummer's day are there?"

"That's the easy bit, sire; we simply concoct a believable attempt on your life. No actual danger to yourself of course, but you would then be perfectly entitled to want to give thanks at the major temples in both Rome and Zampetta."

"Okay. But who will provide us with the necessary scapegoat for the failed attempt? It would be too obvious if it was in any way closely linked to Crastus or Galerius."

"The obvious candidate that springs to mind is the Princess Hera Agrippina. Ever since your divorce, she has been intriguing to keep her son as the heir to the throne and, by all accounts, is becoming more desperate, since your twins are now of an age to inherit. One of those intrigues can provide the pretext we want at the time of our choosing."

Valerian dismissed Gaius and sat in thought for a long time. The subtlety of Gaius's proposal definitely appealed to him and afforded the opportunity to prune another branch of his often fractious family. He mused over the idea of implicating Crastus with the princess's supposed plot but, in the end, dismissed this as an idea. Crastus was too far away to be actively involved with a palace plot, and in any case was publicly well known for his distaste for palace intrigues. Anyway, his very public humiliation by the then-empress some twenty odd years ago would render such a liaison improbable.

Satisfied with his plans, he signalled one of the waiting attendants. The young blonde approached him and at his signal gracefully dropped the golden gossamer tunic, which was her only garment, to the floor and sank to her knees to do his bidding.

Whilst the girl kept his body occupied, he quickly read the rest of the report and noted that the number of casualties was already in excess of his own military advisers' estimates. This was particularly true of both the Seventh and Seventeenth legions whilst Crastus's Fifth seemed relatively intact. The supply consumption rate was high as well. Under normal circumstances, Valerian would not be worried about that, he was happier for his generals to spend arrows and projectiles rather than trained men.

Rome could certainly better afford the former than the latter.

Chapter 21 - Gabrielle

Blissfully unaware of the machinations in Rome over a hundred miles to the West, Crastus continued to plan his next move. The quick successes by Schonberg's assaults had presented him with a double-edged sword of both risk and opportunity.

His back creaking from hours spent bent over the sand table model, he stretched and sent one of his orderlies to locate Leander and Maximus.

When his two closest confidants arrived, he lost no time in outlining his plan.

"We need to maintain the momentum we now have. Both the Seventh and especially the Seventeenth need to have a few more days to rest and restructure after the losses of the last few days. Therefore, the only formation we can use to attack with is the Fifth. Given the relative dispositions of the legion at the moment, we are going to have to attack Gabrielle."

Maximus winced. The level of firepower displayed from the very walls he was being told to attack had been higher than expected during the diversionary attack a couple of weeks earlier. Now, the fortress had been reinforced further and the army commander was based there as well. That was bound to make the defenders fight harder still.

The less experienced Leander was more optimistic. Having been kept close to his mentor throughout the campaign so far, did this now mean he was going to take an active part in the forthcoming battle?

Crastus dashed his impetuous aide's hopes instantly.

"Leander, I want you to take the plan of attack over to Claudius and stay with him to help organise the assistance I will be asking for."

Seeing the crestfallen look on the young man's face Crastus continued,

"Don't worry, you'll get your chance at glory soon enough.

"I do not intend to assault the south wall directly. This failed against Dominique and I do not want to take those kinds of casualties again. The curtain wall meets Gabrielle about a third of the way along the South wall. This is a weak point. I want to use the curtain wall as a shield to prevent the troops manning the western wall from hitting the approach routes."

Maximus nodded thoughtfully.

"If I was to sneak the Second and Fifth cohorts into AnnMarie overnight, they would probably assume that we were going to attack Isabelle. That's right, my friend, we'll take them in quite openly through the breach. The troops already within AnnMarie will start harassing Isabelle just before dawn. The Second cohort will silently pass back out through the breach and, hidden by the walls of AnnMarie mass at the corner nearest Gabrielle. Most of the Fifth will follow as soon as the Second launch their attack. Two centuries of the Fifth will deploy onto the curtain wall as soon as the Second are spotted. They will draw as much of the fire from the west wall and tower as possible. Meanwhile the Sixth cohort will advance to within range of the south wall to provide covering fire. The acute angle of the attack will mean the defenders on the south wall will be exposing themselves to fire so the Sixth should get some good pickings."

For the first time, Leander realized his commander was organising an attack without coordinating it with either of the other legion commanders. Knowing he had just received dispatches from Rome, he began to realise just how much pressure was being exerted on his commander from on high.

"The orders are written up. Leander, take this copy to Claudius and stay with him as per your orders. Maximus, get a courier to take this copy to Schonberg. I do not want you to lead the Second into the attack. I want you marshalling our troops from the tower in AnnMarie and, if the attack looks like it's not going to succeed, I want you to sound the recall. We attack at first light."

* * * *

The preparations carried on through the night. Leander felt the full weight of Claudius's disapproval, but was pleasantly surprised when Claudius spent over an hour pouring over the maps with his own staff looking for ways to help divide the enemy's attention. The master of deception was hard at work. Dawn broke and Leander could hear the cries of alarm as the attacking forces were spotted. Claudius launched two cohorts at Isabelle in a furious pell-mell attack whose only purpose was to ensure that enemy attention was divided. For ten to fifteen minutes, the Seventh distracted the forces within Isabelle who might otherwise have attempted to interfere with the Fifth's attack or launch a spoiling or counter attack.

Schonberg was also hard at work. His troops lined the walls of the city facing Gabrielle and his men poured devastating fire onto the North or nearest wall of the fortress. The city gates crashed open and the whirl of activity that could be viewed inside convinced the defenders that an attack along the causeway was imminent.

The Fifth's attack had been spotted immediately after the first men rounded the tower on the corner of AnnMarie. For once, the sentries posted by the defenders were alert. The leading centuries of the Second cohort charged forward, keeping as close to the foot of the curtain wall as possible. Defensive fire began to rain down from the westernmost tower of Gabrielle and casualties began to fall. They were almost half way when the troops on the southern wall began to fire as well. This was what the Sixth cohort had been waiting for. Their top archers had infiltrated closer to the fortress during the night and now began to pick off the men who had to expose themselves to fire obliquely along the wall.

Meanwhile, the two hundred or so men detailed from the Fifth cohort had been lowered on ropes down onto the curtain wall. They formed a wall of shields and advanced along the top of the wall, albeit some considerable distance behind the troops on the ground. The men at the foot of the wall were now past the foot of the tower and the scaling ladders were being run forwards as they approached the junction of the curtain wall with the fortress itself.

The problem with attacking on such a narrow front was that it gave the defenders a narrow target to strike back against. Strike back they did. Suddenly, several large jugs of kerosene came flying over the parapet. Each jug broke on impact, covering the ground with the highly flammable liquid. Several more followed and finally, a volley of torches followed.

Since there had been no rain for over a week, the grass outside the fortress, dry before it was drenched in the kerosene, caught immediately. The first five or six ranks of the assaulting troops were caught in the conflagration as the kerosene coating them burst into flame. They recoiled and ran in several directions. Some ran out into the open, but many turned and ran back into the advancing ranks of their compatriots. The sudden shock of the fire bursting in front of them coupled with the appearance of man shaped burning comets charging into their midst was unnerving for the remaining troops. They at first halted, and then collectively turned and retreated back the way they had come.

The attack had been broken almost as soon as it had begun. Two entire centuries of the Second cohort had been wiped out, the luckiest of them being those wounded in the early part of the attack. The exposed troops of the Fifth cohort stranded on the curtain wall caught a huge volume of fire before they were able to retreat and in the shadow of AnnMarie drop to ground level. With no one left to support them, the Sixth slowly retreated out of range and the other diversionary forces wound down.

Crastus had been given a very bloody nose.

Chapter 22 - Beatrice

By late the following morning, the three legion commanders had arrived at a consensus with a plan that appeared to offer the best possible way forward. They remained unwilling to attack the strongly defended Isabelle and Eliane, and Gabrielle was by far the strongest of the remaining fortresses. Gabrielle was also obviously the most ably commanded of the four, given the rebuff suffered by Crastus. That left Beatrice and the only decision left had been to decide how to go about it.

Over the next couple of days, Actas's men would be recalled from their patrolling in order to bolster the defensive perimeter. As they came in, they would take over the positions held by Claudius's Seventh facing Isabelle and, as these were relieved, they would move out of sight of the fortresses, circle behind Crastus's own Fifth and cross the downstream fords before marching up to Beatrice from the East. These fords were only passable because of the water dammed up behind the sluice gates meant the downstream river level was much lower than usual. Meanwhile, the remainder of Schonberg's troops on the north bank would thin themselves out even more, and a complete cohort would be placed at the extreme left of their line to act as a reserve for Claudius. Crastus's Fifth would also reduce the garrison within AnnMarie and take over these duties within Dominique as well. The plan would release five full cohorts of the Seventh for the assault on Beatrice.

At the same time, the engineering troops of the Fifth, under Maximus, would dig approach earthworks towards the front and eastern corner of Gabrielle and move the catapults and ballistae forward so that they were close to Gabrielle but, more importantly, able to fire across the river at Beatrice too.

All three men had been concerned at the supply situation leading up to the capture of the city. They had already expended over one hundred thirty thousand arrows and most of their black powder stores. Other critical stores had been low although food and fodder was rarely going to be a problem within Italy's east coast fertile plains. During that day, however, two important wagon convoys had arrived bringing a large amount of stores especially arrows and medical supplies.

With his part in the coming operations agreed, Schonberg excused himself and left to make the perilous return trip into the city to take command there. Crastus and Claudius continued their conference as they tried to finalize an attack plan which would give them the best chance of success with the least number of casualties.

The problem for Claudius was by no means trivial, approaching from the downstream side of the fortress was attacking uphill and the potential covering fire from Gabrielle would be withering on his flank as he did so. They had considered a further river borne diversionary attack against Beatrice but dismissed this as it would have been subjected to a murderous crossfire from Beatrice, Eliane and Gabrielle. With any retreat being against the current, it had been rejected as suicidal.

Not only was the assault uphill but the runoff from Schonberg's diversionary trench had soaked the ground to the north of his approach. The resultant boggy ground prevented him taking a wider route, which would have kept his forces out of range of the troops in Gabrielle.

As much as they both hated the idea of another set piece frontal assault, neither man could come up with a different plan.

The best plan of attack seemed to centre on keeping the forces within Gabrielle as fully involved with defending themselves for as long as possible rather than rushing to help their comrades. Such a deception would be very difficult to perpetrate given that the eastern or downriver approach to Beatrice yielded no cover for over two miles. Once Claudius's assault troops came into view, there was no chance of concealing their numbers from the defenders in daylight. Needing a minimum of thirty minutes to cover the open ground in full kit and carrying scaling equipment, there would be ample time for the defenders to react. This left no options but for a night attack.

A mass night attack was not something either general favoured. The Roman army in general preferred to fight in daylight so that the commanders could control the battle as much as possible. At night, the risks of losing control of the battle and thereby converting a victory into a massive defeat were magnified and multiplied. Small scale surprise attacks, such as those used to capture both AnnMarie and Claudine, were one thing, but the chances of doing this against Beatrice were too slim to contemplate.

Crastus now saw, with the difficult decisions behind them, the sheer brilliance of Claudius in action. They moved to Crastus' more austere tent and positioned themselves around the sand table model.

"This is how I want it to unfold," said Claudius. "Starting tomorrow and continuing for the next three days and two nights, I want the catapults ringing Gabrielle to bombard both forts. I want continuous harassing fire without letup. Whilst some of the catapults are being moved, the rest are firing. When those are emplaced, they take up the strain whilst the others leapfrog forwards."

Crastus nodded in turn. "That way the entire garrison of Gabrielle should be worn out with the strain of the bombardment and also the need to keep standing watch."

"That's right, Crastus. I also want at least one cohort of your Fifth to constantly keep feinting against Gabrielle's walls so that they have to stand to in case the feint develops into a full scale attack. They don't have to do much or take big risks; they are doing their job simply by keeping the walls manned. Flavius has to respond each time just in case."

"Good, and if we get Schonberg to do the same against both Eliane and Beatrice we'll keep them off-balance and tired too. Both he and I will rotate which troops we use and vary the point of the probing attack, as a result they'll have to react."

"That's a good idea, by the end of the third day they should be tired and we both know tired men make mistakes. My Seventh will be well rested by then having taken no part in the action of the next three days and having marched off in small units over the three days it should not be obvious that they are no longer confronting Isabelle."

Claudius paused and looked at his commander. "You know, the thing I really don't understand is why the defenders have been so passive. If you or I had been defending this place there would have been many more counter-attacks and spoiling attacks rather than passively sitting still and waiting for our move. I know Flavius is inexperienced, but he is not a complete tyro. He must know this."

" I agree , and we must be ready in case he suddenly grows a backbone and a brain, but I am more inclined to believe that he intends to hang onto as many of the forts for as long as possible to deny Valerian the chance to enter the city. Someone over there must be aware of our timetable and Valerian's plans. If they can keep Gabrielle at least until after the solstice, they will have effectively denied Valerian his victory."

"You think he's thinking along those lines?"

"I can find no other rationale behind his reluctance to come out and fight. He must be looking for some kind of political settlement once he has effectively defeated Valerian's most able commanders."

The self-depreciating smile Crastus flashed at Claudius to accompany his comments was met by an equally rueful one.

"I don't think he's quite that smart, do you?" asked Claudius as he continued to stare at the sand box model.

"Who knows?"

Claudius picked up his pointer and tapped the sand just outside the middle of the eastern wall of Beatrice.

"This is my attack point, I think. It will be difficult for the tower guards to accurately target my men as they attack, and the slight cover afforded by the way the tower juts out will keep Flavius's men in Gabrielle from directly targeting the men on the ladders as they climb. If I can get my men to the foot of the wall, or at least nearly there, before the alarm sounds then we have a good chance."

"One last question. Claudius, you wanted a better preparation bombardment before attacking Dominique last time. Are you sure you don't want the same here, and are you sure that you don't want another of your trademark multi-stage diversions?"

"That's cheating, that's two questions not one." Claudius grinned. "Flavius knows that if the attack is to come against Gabrielle, then it will be from the Fifth and straight in. If they notice I've moved away, they will suspect the same type of attack that took Dominique. This way, a night assault from the Seventh will be the unexpected move."

The conference broke up and both commanders began their preparations.

* * * *

After three days of incessant, small scale attacks, as evening fell, everybody was in position. Crastus's catapult teams were nearly seventy yards closer to the walls of Gabrielle and had needed to construct some high earthworks to protect the crews from direct fire by men on those walls. The unremitting twang of the catapults and crash of the landing projectiles had hopefully frayed the nerves of the defenders. Crastus was pleased to hear alarm calls going out within the walls even when the feinting attacks weren't being mounted. The troops within Gabrielle were definitely on edge. This had a downside to it; the fact that the sentries were jumpy might allow then to spot Claudius's approach too soon.

When night fell, the catapults one by one shifted their aim points and remained silent. Only three were still aimed at Gabrielle and they were now firing at full pelt as if the whole battery was still aiming there. Crastus and the rest of the besiegers waited anxiously as Claudius's force crept silently closer. At night, in a silent attack, there was no way for Claudius to signal his progress to Crastus. Crastus had placed a number of observers along the river bank with orders to return and report once the force on the other bank drew closer; but the closer they got, the further they actually angled away from the river.

Finally, a thin cry of alarm sounded from the top of the wall facing Claudius. It carried easily in the still night air. Crastus waited a few seconds to be sure it wasn't a false alarm but, as the hubbub grew on the walls facing Claudius, it was obvious that the attack had been spotted. Surprise now lost, Crastus gave the orders and immediately the rested catapult crews sprang into action. Seven projectiles arched their way over the top of Gabrielle and smashed into the south east tower of Beatrice. Three minutes later, a further set of projectiles arched up and then independent fire almost ensured there was at least one boulder in the air at all times. Crastus had moved a couple of the ballistae up close to the river bank and these now began raining bundles of arrows at the top of the river wall of Gabrielle in an attempt to suppress covering fire from there. The three remaining catapults were quickly spiked round and began aiming at the north-eastern tower of Gabrielle and their incendiary projectiles soon added their lurid glow to the scene unfolding in front of them.

The burning trails of the incendiaries and the light from the small fires started in the vicinity of the tower, as well as a lookout beacon on the top, ignited by a very lucky first shot, illuminated the scene across the river.

Claudius had indeed managed to get his troops very close to the wall before that first alarm call. Now, as the defenders raced to react, his men were already at the foot of the wall.

In the darkness, neither commander could be sure of precisely what was happening. Crastus had the advantage; he knew what was supposed to happen. Flavius could still not be certain that this was not a feint to draw his troops away from the front walls of Gabrielle. There was no way to be sure and, caught between two equally difficult choices, he stood fast and kept the troops that could have reinforced Beatrice within Gabrielle instead.

The first troops up the ladders met fierce opposition. But in a night attack, with the interior of the fortress lit and the attackers coming from darkness into light, the advantages were all with the attackers– except for numbers. Here, they were at the disadvantage. The chances of the first man up the ladder surviving was minimal, the chance of the second only slightly better. The survival chance of the fiftieth was much better still.

The ferocity of the fighting on the wall could only be dimly observed. The defenders quickly learned that ground once grudgingly given up could not usually be recaptured. The little pools of attackers linked up and the force coalesced. Soon, the bulk of the wall was in the hands of the Seventh and men were beginning to fight their way down inside.

Just as with the other fortresses, as soon as the main defensive wall was breached and the sphere of conflict widened, it appeared that the heart went out of the defenders. Ground began to be conceded at an ever greater rate and the end was very soon in sight.

Ninety minutes later, the fortress was in Claudius's hands. Most of the remaining defenders had fled through the passages of the linking wall into Gabrielle. Three of the four towers were abandoned to the Seventh and only the southern river tower with its link to Gabrielle and the gatehouse held out. The gatehouse surrendered when they saw they had no hope of escape in any direction and Claudius himself led the storming attack that took the last tower.

Claudius had blocked his end of the passageways which, given their constricted size, were relatively easy to blockade and defend and, by first light, the fortress, captured relatively undamaged, was secure.

Another of the Seven Sisters had fallen. Only three remained.

Chapter 23 - Rome

The news of Crastus's rushed attack on Gabrielle and its subsequent failure came as no surprise to Gaius. The news, hard on its heels, of the successful capture of Beatrice was. Gaius was now in a quandary. His position in the palace enabled him to protect some of his relatives with ease, one or two with more difficulty, but Crastus was now a real problem to the family. His near stellar successes with the army made him an easy target for the jealousy that was rife in the political environment of the palace. A minor defeat was actually personally good news for Crastus, even if he didn't know it. The storming of the other river fort, Beatrice was on the other hand not so good.

Gaius would have to work fast. Already the report would have found its way to Valerian and the number of hands it would have passed through on the way would ensure it was public knowledge within the hour. Some vacuous, empty headed courtier would be bound to offer his congratulations to Crastus via the throne during the audiences today. Such a move would probably spark Valerian's temper and the insanely jealous and paranoid emperor could act precipitously.

The arrival two days ago of the extremely young Scipio Africanus, the only surviving son of the Pretender would need to be used to deter Valerian. The poor boy, not yet into his man's growth, was doomed anyway. Gaius' mind raced.

Within three hours the purse of gold changed hands no less than five times before it reached the necessarily venal guard. The third person handling it never saw the blade that removed him from any chance of confessing his part in the affair. The highly expendable servant was expended.

There were always three guards watching the young prisoner and, to prevent collusion, were drawn from three different units of the Praetorian Guard. This practice had been in place for hundreds of years when guarding the most important prisoners for the Emperor. Unfortunately for the officers concerned, it had been circumvented for just as long.

The chosen bribed guard had paid off the other two men, whom he knew well and at the prearranged signal plunged his sword through the chest of the startled and frightened young prisoner. At his later interrogation, the man would insist that he was sure the boy was trying to say thank you as he fell. It didn't save the guard. He died under the questioning.

* * * *

Gaius hurried to the dressing room behind the throne end of the audience chamber. It was very unusual for anyone to interrupt Valerian here. Not only did he use the room to put on the robes of state but also, via one of the numerous nubile palace slaves, he used an age old method to relieve the tension. This was precisely what he was doing when Gaius burst into the room waving the report of what had transpired in the palace dungeons.

Quite literally in mid act, the Emperor listened to Gaius' report without comment. He dismissed the luckless slave who gratefully and gracefully bowed her way out. She, in her naivety, did not expect that the soldiers Gaius had brought along for this purpose had instructions to dispose of her body quietly.

When they were alone, Valerian allowed his temper to boil.

"Who did this?"

"We do not as yet know, Sire. The assassin was one of the Praetorian guards and he died under questioning. We have the name of the man who paid him, but he is a notorious go-between and will have gone to ground."

The emperor glowered at his chamberlain.

"And what am I supposed to do about it?"

"Patience, Sire. I am sure we will run the truth down soon enough. The boy was no threat and I am sure that the perpetrators will be brought to justice before too long."

Of course Gaius, secure in his knowledge, intended to ensure that the Princess Hera would be implicated, but that revelation would wait for a short time yet.

"I have taken the liberty of cancelling your audiences for today, Sire."

Valerian had been expecting that and, although he suspected Gaius was manoeuvring him, he had not a shred of evidence.

"What about Zampetta? It looks like your cousin is going to succeed."

"It seems very much that way, Sire. The three garrisons left are unable to support each other and I doubt that any of them will have much of a stomach for a fight now. Do you want me to continue with the preparations for bringing your pilgrimage forwards?"

"Yes, I think so; I want to get out of this treacherous city!"

Gaius wisely bowed and left, happy that he had managed to head off any confrontation over Crastus and at the same time having assured that his distant cousin's unfortunate offspring had at least met a quick end. Now, he could fabricate the evidence that would implicate Hera.

Yes, all in all, a good day.

Chapter 24 - Gabrielle

Dawn after the fall of Beatrice found Crastus pondering the solution to his next problem. He now had three pockets of enemy resistance isolated from each other. None of them were in range of being able to provide covering fire for each other, none of them could communicate directly, although flag signals could be seen passing information and orders from one to the other.

Eliane was relatively weak and isolated as it was on the wrong side of the river, Crastus felt he could pick that one of at will. Isabelle and Gabrielle were entirely different propositions. Until the machinery within Gabrielle was his, he could not bring the flooding level around the city under control so the city side approaches to both fortresses were under water accept for the narrow causeways. He could not assault such a fortress on a narrow front which was only wide enough for six soldiers side by side.

The passageways connecting Beatrice to Gabrielle were even narrower and he was sure that the defenders would have adequately manned defences in place there, just as Claudius had on his side in Beatrice. This left the outer walls again. Following the successful attacks on AnnMarie, Claudine and Beatrice by night, he was reasonably certain that any night moves would be vulnerable with the attackers ready for them. This left a daylight assault on Gabrielle's outside walls. It appeared to be the Fifth's turn to fight and die again.

A commotion at the entrance to Crastus's tent broke into his thoughts. He could hear his intelligence officer, Gaius, demanding entrance. Signalling the guards to let him in, he was still unprepared for the extremely dirty apparition before him. Gaius was absolutely filthy, covered from head to toe in dirt, dust and by the smell, something far worse. It was this latter covering that had prompted his guards to refuse him entry. His normally quite fastidious mannerisms were often the point of jokes within the officer's mess, but this was the opposite.

Gaius was almost hopping in excitement as he started to report but prudently kept three or four yards away from Crastus.

"We've found it!" he yelled exultantly.

"Found what?" Crastus asked, eyebrow raised.

"Do you remember the rumour we tried to track down five years ago when we were last here?"

"Which rumour?"

"The tunnel one!"

Comprehension now dawned for Crastus.

"Five years ago, we were told of the rumour of the existence of a tunnel connecting Gabrielle to the city – is that the one you mean?"

"Yes!" Gaius was exultant.

"It's there, it exists, and it's even still in good repair even though nobody has used it for over seventy years. I've just spent an hour listening to Flavius' cooks complaining in the kitchens in the basements of Gabrielle!"

"So that's why you're covered in shit."

"No, they're not quite cooking with that just yet . . ." Gaius trailed off as he realized Crastus had not intended to be taken literally. He began again,

"True, it's not clean down there, but we can take Gabrielle from the inside through it. The tunnel comes up within the fortress basement within ten paces of the entrance to Beatrice and only fifteen paces from the wheel room and less than that from the inner river tower. If we can get a sufficient force in there, we can take all three before they know what's hit them and Claudius's troops can swarm across whilst the rest of the Fifth come over the wall."

"And you're sure they don't know about it?"

"Absolutely. No one had been down there before us in living memory. We only found it by chance because one of the local stonemasons remembered something his grandfather once said. For once, I had the time to track it down and, suddenly, we had found the city end behind a wall in the basement of a merchant's house in the eastern corner of the city. Luckily, this building wasn't damaged when we took the city. They know nothing about it or they would have used it before now, particularly while we were still weak just after taking the city."

"How many troops would you need to take the passageway into Gabrielle and the winding room?"

"About a hundred and fifty. If Claudius is ready to send more across the river immediately, we can expand out from there easily enough."

"How long to set it up?"

"Half a day, we could certainly move tomorrow."

Crastus turned to his writing table and quickly wrote up the sets of orders instructing the necessary officers as to their parts in the upcoming operation. Schonberg would detach two centuries under Gaius's leadership to approach through the tunnel. Claudius would have two cohorts ready to assault across the river as soon as Gaius had captured the Gabrielle end of the connecting passageways over the river. Meanwhile, Maximus would lead four cohorts of the Fifth in a frontal attack on the eastern wall of the fortress.

* * * *

The Italian spring climate remained true as the following day dawned clear and bright. By mid-morning, it was obvious to Flavius and his staff that the Fifth intended to attack. The four attacking cohorts had drawn themselves up into the straightforward, broad assault formation and the catapults were concentrating on the defences nearest to them. The catapult range was so short that they were able to fire their missiles in very high trajectories to land them almost vertically onto the top of the eastern wall. Accordingly, having ensured that the other walls were reasonably manned and that the passageway across to Beatrice was fully defended, Flavius put as many of his troops as possible ready to defend the threatened eastern wall.

The attack came in on the established pattern. The attacking troops ran forward carrying scaling ladders and grappling hooks. At the edge of arrow range, fully a third of the attackers stopped, unlimbered their shields and their bows and commenced withering fire at the wall top. Flavius had, however, placed a larger number of his troops within the towers this time and their return fire was extremely accurate from well-protected positions. The Fifth's casualties mounted quickly even before the first troops reached the wall. It certainly looked that the attack was never going to carry the wall on its own. Flavius, suspecting a trick similar to one of those to which his other forts had succumbed, looked around but no other threat materialised.

Unbeknown to Flavius, at that very moment, nearly two hundred of Schonberg's men had used the tunnel to enter the basements in the north west corner of the fort and were about to attack his blocking troops at the entrance to Beatrice from behind.

Those troops had very little chance. On the first level, one of the cooks had managed to shout a warning and the men turned from the barricade to face the onslaught just in time. A short, ugly fight ensued in the semi-darkness of the passageway, but the numbers were too uneven and the Seventeenth carried the day. One level up, the defenders had no warning and the first thing they knew about the enemy behind them was a volley of arrows that dropped three quarters of them instantly. One huge sergeant held four of the attackers at bay until two archers put arrows into him and then both passageways were clear.

On each level, three quick blasts of a trumpet, the agreed signal, were heard and quickly the men of the Seventh began to pour through across the river having already quietly removed their barricades.

Meanwhile, in the winding room, two groups of men of about equal numbers were now playing a deadly game of cat and mouse between and around the equipment with one group attempting to deny the other control of the machinery.

With no quarter being asked or given, the fight quickly degenerated into a flurry of hand to hand individual contests. When the Seventeenth's men were reinforced by their comrades from the Seventh who had seized the passageways across the river, this, too, became a foregone conclusion.

With opposition behind them eliminated, the Seventeenth began to spread out through the interconnected cellars and basements of the fortress whilst the Seventh massed near the north western tower ready to attack as soon as the alarm was given. Despite the noise engendered by the short and brutal fights within the rooms at that end of fortress, the noise of the assault on the wall drowned out the other sounds. Eventually, this came to an end as a startled sentry gave the alarm.

Flavius turned from the fight where a few of the Fifth had gained the top of the wall and stared down into the body of the fortress at the cry. There, unbelievably, he could see the Seventh charging for the base of the tower, the doorway to which was not only open but also unguarded. Several small units of the Seventh were also charging across the courtyard, aiming for other strategic points. He was further stunned when men of the Seventeenth suddenly burst out of the buildings almost immediately below him. Men all along the wall faltered at the sight behind them and that few seconds allowed enough men of the Fifth to gain the wall. At that moment, the tide turned decisively and the fortress was lost. Singly and then in increasing numbers the embattled defenders on the eastern wall began to throw down their swords and surrender. Men of the Seventh burst through the tower top on the inside tower and raised their banner. The inside of the fortress was in Crastus's hands and the other walls were being raked with arrow fire. With no inner parapet, there was little or no cover for the defenders and they fell in windrows. Within three minutes, all Flavius's forces held were three disconnected towers and, even as he watched, he saw another assault team carry the doorway into the other river tower.

He was beaten and he hadn't even raised his own sword. in anger at that point. He moved to the edge of the tower and looked over. The sheer drop was certainly enough and, saluting the one tribune who had stayed with him throughout, simply leaned out over the edge and let himself fall.

On seeing their commander fall, the fight went out of the rest of the men defending Gabrielle and, in turn, each tower surrendered, just as they had with the other fortresses. Gabrielle had fallen, too.

Only two Sisters remained.

Chapter 25 - Valerian

Back in Rome, unaware that events had moved so precipitously and triumphantly forwards, Valerian still mused over a strategy that would give him everything he wanted. He needed the last army of the Pretender to be defeated, he needed to make good his boast of spending the solstice in Zampetta and he needed Crastus to come out of the campaign smelling of something other than roses.

He had delayed a couple of re-supply wagon convoys a few days in order to increase the pressure, but was unwilling to do much more than this. He was, therefore, not in a very good mood when Gaius Flavius interrupted his chain of thought. The man marched into the otherwise empty audience chamber with a very large Praetorian Guard escort.

Before he could stammer out a challenge to this unprecedented intrusion, Gaius announced

"My lord, forgive the imposition but we have come at once bearing grave news. There was a plot within the palace to assassinate you this very morning!"

Valerian stared as the front rank of the Praetorians parted.

There held between two of the guards, in chains, and with the obvious signs of a struggle visible on her bare arms, stood his first wife, the Princess Hera Agrippina. Divorced soon after the birth of his first son because she could bear him no more, the royal princess had spent twenty years under house arrest within the palace and, although treated with respect, had often been accused of plots against him. Never, however, had these accusations been taken seriously. Now it seemed his chamberlain had gone a whole lot further.

"Have you taken leave of your senses?" Valerian asked although the sly look on his face confirmed to the princess that he was more aware than the feigned surprise showed. "She is a Princess of the royal blood. She should never be treated this way. Remove those chains and let her stand before me."

The commander of the Praetorians bowed and approaching the princess held out the key and she meekly extended each arm in turn to allow the chains to be removed. As the last chain fell away, she bowed to her former husband and said,

"My lord, please allow me the time to present myself to you properly. I am not attired for these surroundings." Indeed she wasn't, she wore only the thin nightgown she had worn to bed where she had been apprehended.

On getting no reply, she stepped forwards and bowed again, then stood chin outthrust, her proud bearing eloquent testimony to the fact that she was every inch an Imperial princess.

"My lord, we have concrete proof that an assassin was smuggled into the palace as one of the princess's servants and we in fact apprehended him within twenty yards of your sleeping chamber this morning. Luckily, you were with one of the concubines at the time." Gaius at least had the decency to look embarrassed at this last.

"He sang like a canary once the questionarii had him tied down. We interviewed the princess's own chamberlain this morning and he has confirmed the salient facts. He implicated the princess herself and, for your safety, she was taken into custody. She, however, declines to confirm these details."

"You put a Princess of the Blood Royal to the question?"

"Nay, Sire. That is forbidden. The princess struggled with the guards and they had to use a modicum of force to restrain her."

At this, the accused woman jerked her head up and stared boldly at her former husband. She already knew there was no hope for her; such an accusation could only result in one end. The only question was whether Valerian would grant her a quick death or would indulge his widely known streak of inventive cruelty.

"Do you have anything to say to me?" the emperor asked in a surprisingly mild tone of voice.

When she did not deign to answer, he looked at her for a few seconds as if appraising a piece of meat.

He stepped down from the dais and circled her. Coming again to a position directly in front of her, he stared into her still beautiful face for a moment. She stared haughtily back; no one would be able to say that Hera Agrippina did not meet her fate full in the face. Again, he stepped behind her and this time he saw the slight tensing of her shoulder muscles as she appeared to guess his intentions. He took the ceremonial dagger from its sheath silently and with a sudden and quick motion sliced the single shoulder strap of the thin nightdress she wore. The ruined garment fluttered to the floor leaving her exposed to the eyes of all present. Even though she was now approaching forty, her skin remained flawless, her figure near perfect despite having borne the emperor a son..

Still, she did not move, merely shivering slightly in the slight chill morning breeze that disturbed the room.

"Kneel."

Gracefully she sank to her knees on the ruins of her clothing and sank back onto her haunches without once using her hands. It was now obvious what her former husband intended. Still, she would not yield.

Having put the dagger away the Emperor gestured to the guard commander who handed over his razor sharp sword.

Poised behind her, he gazed down on the flawless beauty of his former wife.

The strike came without warning. They all knew his intention and her position and passivity showed she was equally aware of her fate. The sword flashed up and then down. The point entered her shoulder just behind the collar bone and in front of the shoulder bone itself. Angled slightly and avoiding the rib cage the sword tore through the soft tissue of the lungs before spearing through the heart in a moment. The Princess Hera Agrippina died in the space between one heartbeat and the next.

She had died with the hope that this would be the end of it, but the emperor's next words, should she have heard them would have shattered her remaining illusion and she would have died in true despair.

"Bring me the child of this piece of carrion, and bring me a garrotting cord."

Soon there would only be two sons to choose between when it became time to pass the crown on.

Interfering with Crastus's campaign was now forgotten.

"Prepare for the pilgrimage. We ride for Zampetta in two days."

Chapter 26 - Eliane

Crastus had been somewhat relieved to hear the casualty figures from the taking of Gabrielle. There had been just fewer than two hundred fatalities and only slightly more than that wounded. Although the Fifth had taken the bulk of these, and despite the casualties from the earlier attempt, it was still the strongest of the three legions.

Now there were only two fortresses left to reduce. Isolated Eliane on the north bank and Isabelle, both surrounded on all four sides. Both had substantial garrisons, but the total number of troops left did not equate to a single full legion. Neither fortress was in a position to cover the other, whilst Crastus was confident that he had sufficient forces to reduce both.

There was no real choice; they had to take Eliane first – it was the weaker of the two remaining bastions and the storming of Isabelle was going to need the heavy equipment that would take a couple of days at least to move from its current positions facing the now-captured Gabrielle.

With his troops already in place facing Eliane from three sides, it logically fell to Schonberg to take Eliane. The big German was not in the mood for any more subtlety so proposed a simple attack on both the outer and inner walls. He intended to use grappling hooks thrown from rafts to pull down the known weak inner wall and then, using the rest of the rafts from the earlier river assault, to cross the river from the city and enter through the breach. At the same time, his outer troops would attack the north wall in much the same way as Maximus had attacked Gabrielle.

Crastus reviewed the plan with his fellow commander and gave it his approval; the only bone of contention had been the timing of the attack. Schonberg wanted to attack that very afternoon. This was an argument that Crastus eventually won by insisting that a dawn attack would work better as there was no artillery preparation to coordinate.

* * * *

The following morning was unusually misty for the season, but that suited Schonberg. With muffled paddles, the lead rafts ghosted across the sluggish current. The first the defenders knew about the attack was when the ropes whistled over the parapet and the grapples ground their points into the inside of the wall. The attacking troops knew that the wall was weak due to lack of maintenance, but just how weak was demonstrated much more quickly than had been anticipated. The ropes attached to the grapples did not stretch back to the rafts but instead all the way back to the wharves on the other side of the river. Here the other ends had been attached to teams of horses who were rapidly walked away from the river to take up the slack. Two of the grapples had not lodged as efficiently as the others and simply pulled free. The other four were more than enough to do the job. With a series of resounding crashes, the wall came crashing down into the knee high water outside the fortress. The breach in the wall of Eliane had taken all of five minutes to achieve and, since the covering fire from the towers had been non-existent, it had been achieved at no loss.

Outside the complex to the north, Schonberg's other units came storming across the earthwork and ditch and rapidly approached the foot of the wall. Still, no defensive fire came. The troops flung their ladders up and mounted them as fast as they could. Meanwhile, the rest of the water borne assault team crossed the river with gusto heading for the pile of jumbled rubble that marked where the wall had stood.

As the first men reached the top of the northern wall and the first of the river crossing reached the gap in the wall, the reason for the absence of defensive fire became apparent. Quickly, the call went out for an officer to come forwards. Schonberg himself went, puzzled by the lack of fighting to be heard. He found his men lined up along the walls of the fortress and the towers already in their hands. Lined up in parade formation but with their shields held over their heads to protect them from incoming fire, was the entire garrison ready to surrender. The officers within Eliane had been whittled down by the desultory diversionary attacks over the intervening time leaving only three centurions to lead the garrison. The most senior centurion left in charge had decided that surrender was the best option rather than fighting on in a lost cause and ordered his men to lay down their weapons at the first sign that the attack was coming in. Schonberg took the fort without any casualties save one poor soul who had broken his leg when he fell in the mad scramble up the ladders and a couple of men who suffered a soaking having had their raft overturned when the wall came down.

Only Isabelle remained.

Chapter 27 - Isabelle

With the exception of the first attacks against Dominique and Gabrielle, each attack had gone so well to plan that Crastus had earned a new nickname – Lucky. Now, however, there remained one more nut to crack, Isabelle. Having been advised by his cousin of the chaos reigning in the palace and that Valerian had moved his schedule up in order to escape from the infighting and was already on his way, Crastus had no more time to lose.

With the surrender without a fight of the garrison of Eliane, he could hope for the same from Isabelle, but all such advances were rebuffed and his heralds were pelted with horse dung from the top of the towers when they approached the main gate.

He needed another day to move his siege equipment into place and then tried again, this time with the whole battery of catapults, ballistae and towers in plain view of the occupants of the fort, but again he was refused a hearing.

Schonberg's troops were now garrisoning the whole of the complex with the exception of AnnMarie. The Fifth garrisoned that one. As the nearest to Isabelle, it would play a part in the attack, and his lines stretched literally to the midpoint of the south wall. The Seventh stretched from there to the walls of Dominique. Between the two legions, they were able to field nearly eleven thousand fit men. Purely for demonstration purposes, Crastus had swelled these numbers by another six hundred by posing all of the walking wounded in the back row. They looked the part from a distance, but would take no part in the actual assault.

For a third and final try he attempted to ask them to surrender. He rode to within twenty paces of the wall. The troops inside could clearly see who it was, his brightly burnished armour and golden horsehair plume identified him even to those who did not know him by sight.

"Solders of Rome! Hear me!"

The age old cry from the commander was normally enough to ensure an audience would at least listen. But not this time, the men inside, even knowing how hopeless their situation was, replied in the same fashion as before. Even though the troops inside knew it wasn't a good idea to pelt a legion commander, let alone one carrying an imperial commission with horse dung, but pelt him they did.

After cleaning up and changing into a clean tunic whilst his servants scrubbed the breastplate clean Crastus dismissed both legions back to watch duties and conferred with his staff.

The intention this time was to bombard the fortress for three days using all of the equipment available and, if necessary, exhausting the ready supplies of ammunition. He was not stupid. He was aware that his supplies were being delayed, probably deliberately, and probably on Valerian's orders, but if they took Isabelle they would not need them. If they didn't, then it wouldn't matter. Valerian would not be able to enter the city and Crastus would be required to personally forfeit his position.

The pounding began. First target was, as before, the stonework atop the walls in order to reduce the cover available for the defenders. Once this had mostly gone, attention was switched to the tower tops until they had also been badly damaged. This took less than a day. There was now no doubt in anyone's mind that all the older fortifications throughout the empire were extremely vulnerable to the more powerful modern catapults.

With the Sky Nest now in place on the far side of AnnMarie and out of range of Isabelle, it had been extended to its full height; the observers could see into the entire fortress. As a result, the fire was now redirected onto individual strong points within the fort until each one was reduced to rubble. The flagmen in the basket were signalling so frantically that they were switched off in relays every two hours. The time spent winching the basket up and down gave the catapult crews a breather but, by the end of each day, the winch crews were worn out too.

With the inside of the fort resembling a smashed rubble-strewn charnel house, it was finally time for the assault to go in.

The following morning revealed to the defenders the same imposing sight that they had seen three days before. Some eight cohorts of fellow legionnaires drawn up in order of battle facing what remained of their south wall. Although not breached, it no longer afforded the full majestic line of defence it hitherto had. The crenulations on the top were gone. In places, the wall was broken down by four or five feet and the even walkway along the top was smashed along its entire length. The four thousand surviving defenders knew that there was no real hope of withstanding such a mass attack. Based on their own actions three days ago, they would at least have to try to withstand it.

Crastus now signalled for the final coup de grâce. The catapults within AnnMarie, having stayed silent throughout the previous three days, now began to fire Crastus's last remaining stores of precious gunpowder. Using the same tactics as before, a set of breaking jugs of black powder followed by an incendiary, explosions began to ring around the confines of the fortress. Cesca was also trying a new trick this time as well. Attached to the incendiary round was a round jug of kerosene which burst on landing adding its flammable liquor to the fire ball. The incendiary effect was out of all proportion to the expenditure of stores and this success was marked down for future use too.

With explosions ringing out at regular intervals which would unnerve most troops, the defenders watched in awe as the massed ranks in front of them, responding to the peal of trumpets, surged forward. There was little point in subtlety. There were no diversionary places to attack, the land around the other three sides of the remaining fortress were draining now, but still flooded to ankle depth and boggy below that. The only route of attack was straight in against the south wall.

Showers of arrows began to rain down as soon as they came into range, but the practiced drills still continued. Answering fire came back as the archers set up. Still, they came on. The fire from the right-hand tower seemed the heaviest, so the signal was flagged to the basket and relayed back to the AnnMarie catapults. Within a scant minute, the explosive bomb sets were detonating in that zone as the aim point of the catapults was changed. The fire slackened, especially after one very lucky set exploded right on the tower top itself reducing the defenders there to flaming pyres.

As the attacking troops reached the foot of the wall, the catapults aim point was switched back to the interior to avoid hitting their own comrades and just as elsewhere the ladders went up quickly.

For the defenders, the age old nightmare unfolded, just as it had in the other fortresses. Too many attacking troops; too much incoming fire and too little cover to return fire from. For once, there were enough men to man all of the defence points and strong points. With inadequate cover for most of these places, casualties mounted very quickly. The expenditure of materiel on both sides was prodigious, but the defenders had less to start with. Soon, the reserves of stores dwindled and the defensive fire slackened. Although Crastus and Claudius were expending their reserves of stores faster, they had far more to start with. This advantage in men and materiel had to tell.

Soon, the lead elements of both legions had gained the wall, linked up and were pushing their perimeter outwards towards the towers and down into the body of the fortress.

When it came, the end came quickly. Just as in Gabrielle the defenders, knowing they had lost, began to surrender. Within minutes, it was all over. The last of the Seven Sisters had fallen.

Chapter 28- Victory

The following morning he called the staff together. The news had arrived during the final assault on Isabelle that Valerian was only two days away. He had brought his schedule forwards and then commenced travelling even in advance of that. With Valerian now due the following day towards evening, it was crucial to return as much of the complex to fully working order as possible.

The worst news was that the breach in AnnMarie was far worse than had been expected. Given the original timetable, Crastus had hoped to repair the breach before Valerian arrived. Unfortunately, the pounding the wall had taken from the barrage had damaged the foundations quite badly.

The sluice gates had been raised three days earlier and the floodwaters were receding quickly. Stone masons had been recruited from within the city, and in partnership with their fellow craftsmen from the three legions were in the process of surveying the damage to the entire complex and preparing a repair program. The major breach in the walls of AnnMarie and the severe damage to the wall tops of Dominique and Isabelle would take weeks and the collapsed wall of Eliane would need replacing from the foundations up.

Meanwhile, smaller jobs could be undertaken. Luckily, the damage to the city had been minor and the palace had been captured intact. First priority was therefore to restore the city to its more normal glory and to start the minor repairs on the other fortresses.

Having no desire to be trapped here himself in the future and certainly not wishing to have any other general mouse trapped into using the same attack routes he had used, he also set out to improve the defences where he could. First order of business was to collapse, flood and fill in the tunnel they had so successfully used to take Gabrielle.

Over the next twenty four hours, the legions, swelled by the number of new recruits hitherto members of the Eleventh, Twelfth and Fourteenth legions, were kept very busy indeed.

* * * *

That evening, a tired but elated staff met in an airy room within the palace complex. For the first time in the siege, Crastus allowed the wine to flow freely undiluted. The earlier celebrations after the capture of AnnMarie, Claudine and especially Dominique paled by comparison. After a couple of hours of sipping politely at his wine and watching his officers develop monstrous hangovers for the morning, Crastus wandered outside. He crossed the grassy hilltop in front of the palace and descended the slight slope to look out over the city.

Below him, the city was a blaze of light from torches on every conceivable wall. Even more twisted snakelike down the roads leading to the river as his jubilant troops sang, and drank and ate and danced through the city. Many of the civilians were out in the streets, too, laughing and joking with their liberators. All of the gates had been thrown open and the celebrations were spilling out onto the causeways connecting the fortresses to the parent city.

Each of the legion commanders had kept a cohort out of the city to man the walls and provide sentries but, in truth, they were really not needed. This had been the last bastion of the army of the Pretender and finally the civil war which had blighted the central Empire for five long years was over. For some reason, and Crastus suspected why, Galerius had never allowed the war to spill over into the provinces. Perhaps he knew, as Crastus suspected, that if the war had escalated out of Italy, the Empire might have fractured just as it had six hundred years ago before Aurelian became emperor. Galerius was not here to see the end of the war. As soon as Galerius had been forced to raise his standard, he would have known that he or Valerian would have to die.

Crastus raised his glass in mute toast to his departed political enemy who had also been a personal friend and under the starry sky pondered what might have happened if he had chosen to take Galerius' offer of command rather than Valerian's.

With that somewhat sombre thought, he turned his back on the thronged city and made his way back inside to join his staff.

Epilogue

The royal party was now two hours away from their destination, the city of Zampetta. As this was the final day of the pilgrimage, Valerian had transferred from his horse drawn opulent carriage to ride the magnificent white charger that had followed behind all the way from Rome.

The emperor was smugly pleased as he rode along. The trumped up plot supposedly by his own eldest son had enabled him to arrest and immediately execute him. As a result, his power-hungry scheming second wife was essentially checkmated and he did not miss the wearisome seventeen-year-old as he had taken an intense personal dislike to him at birth. On top of that, the deliberately false intelligence had led Crastus to assault the Seven Sisters with a much smaller force than prudence would dictate, but he had nevertheless succeeded. That Crastus had asked publicly for more men and Valerian had refused gave credence to the opinions being whispered that Crastus was past it. The fact that he had won a stunning victory could easily be suborned until it would appear to be Valerian's wisdom that had won the day.

Up ahead of the immediate royal bodyguard, the leading elements of the Praetorian Guard closed ranks as the road they followed entered a more heavily wooded section. Normally kept clear for fifty paces on either side of the road, the five years of civil war had allowed scrub to grow more than man high much closer to this. As this was now friendly territory, the guard troops were not particularly alert.

They failed to spot the small party hidden in the scrub. Sabinus, having escaped from the prison transport after early capture by Crastus, had foraged in the woods for days until meeting up with a small group of his own men who had not been satisfied with being inducted into the Fifth and had subsequently deserted. Remembering the former Tribune as a just man, they had quickly formed a mercenary band and were waiting for the chance to jump ship and escape to Greece. Forced inland by heavy patrols from Schonberg's legion and Actas' auxiliaries, they had ended up almost in sight of the Seven Sisters themselves. Hearing the approaching large party, they had been forced to hide rather too close to the road.

The Praetorians passed within yards of the hidden men but did not see them. Sabinus, having spotted the royal banner approaching, used hand signals to inform his men. This was more than just a target of opportunity, but a once in a lifetime chance. All of the men, fiercely loyal to the standards of their own legion, agreed with him. This was a chance to avenge, not just the death of Agrippa and so many of their comrades, but also of the fabled Eleventh legion itself.

As Valerian and his immediate guard rode level with the bushes that concealed them, they rose as one, drew their bows and loosed a fatal flight. One guard, quicker reacting than the rest managed to raise his shield and intercept two arrows with it. A third pitched him lifelessly from his saddle. Two other guards fell, mortally wounded, and two others fought to regain control of their wounded mounts. Valerian, however, was in serious trouble. One arrow struck his horse high in the shoulder and another in the hindquarters. The pain-maddened stallion reared and the emperor, no longer the lithe horseman of his youth was thrown from the saddle. Before the attackers could fire a second volley or before the guards could respond and cut them down, it was over. On falling, Valerian's neck had snapped and he could not feel the smashing force of his horse's hooves as they flailed down on his unprotected body and head. In the few further seconds, the melee continued before all had been cut down the attackers claimed three further guards. Sabinus took no part in this. He simply stood and waited calmly with a smile on his face at his handy-work until the nearest Praetorian simply ran him through.

By the time the badly wounded animal had been put out of its misery, the face of Valerian was unrecognizable and a bloody pulp. If he was to lie in state, as was the way, his face would have to be covered with more than one layer of lace.

The guard commander, ashen faced and knowing by imperial law his own life was forfeit, sent riders galloping ahead to inform the victorious army at the Seven Sisters of the tragedy.

The End

History

As with all stories of alternative history, this one starts with a single event that changes the course of history resulting in an outcome that is radically different from the history which has resulted in our world. They are essentially What If questions written large.

The premise for my story is set six-hundred years before the story takes place.

In 270AD the emperor Aurelian took the throne of Rome. As one of a number of distinguished soldier emperors, he alone would hold the title of 'Restorer of the World'. He successfully defeated a number of rivals for control of the empire and reunited it, expelling a number of barbarian incursions in the process. He commenced the construction of the Aurelian walls around Rome, many parts of which are preserved in good condition and demonstrate the fortress building capabilities of the engineers of the late Roman Empire. He conducted a number of campaigns in the east and brought a fair portion of Asia Minor back under Roman rule. Always known as a stern taskmaster who dealt out vicious punishments for any mistakes or misdemeanours, this would, in our world, be the cause of his downfall.

In 275AD on his way to Persia for another campaign, one of his scribes make a relatively minor mistake. Fearing for his life, he forged a document naming several of the senior officers accompanying Aurelian on his campaign as traitors. These officers, expecting no mercy, then colluded together and murdered Aurelian. Subsequent emperors would eventually prove powerless to stop the partition and final disillusion of the empire itself although this process would take another one-hundred forty years in the west.

What if the plot had failed? This is my branching point.

In the world of this novel, Aurelian was tipped off about the plot by one of the officers who threw himself at his emperor's mercy for something he had not done. Forewarned, Aurelian had the truth tortured out of the scribe and had him impaled for his treachery. Abandoning the campaign in Persia as a preordained failure, Aurelian returned to Rome and spent the next several years consolidating the empire's power and improving both the security of the empire and the lot of its citizens. His successors were able to build on a more stable foundation and as a result the Roman Empire has now thrived for nearly a thousand years.

With such a civilization covering much of Western Europe, the dominant culture in the 9th century AD is exclusively Christian Roman. That veritable stability has produced astonishing inventions and improvements, in particular, military technology which rivals that produced in our world in China at that time.

However, over the last hundred years or so there have been a number of debilitating civil wars and this has severely weakened the central authority in Rome. The worst of these wars, called the Pretender War, has just been won with an epic battle at Salerno where the Pretender's forces were routed and the Pretender himself forced to fall upon his own sword to escape the terrible justice the rightful emperor,

Valerian, would have inflicted upon him. Remnants of his army have retreated to a city near the east coast of Italy, about four miles inland from where the modern city of Pescara now stands. This is how things stood as our story began . . .

Seven Sisters and Zampetta

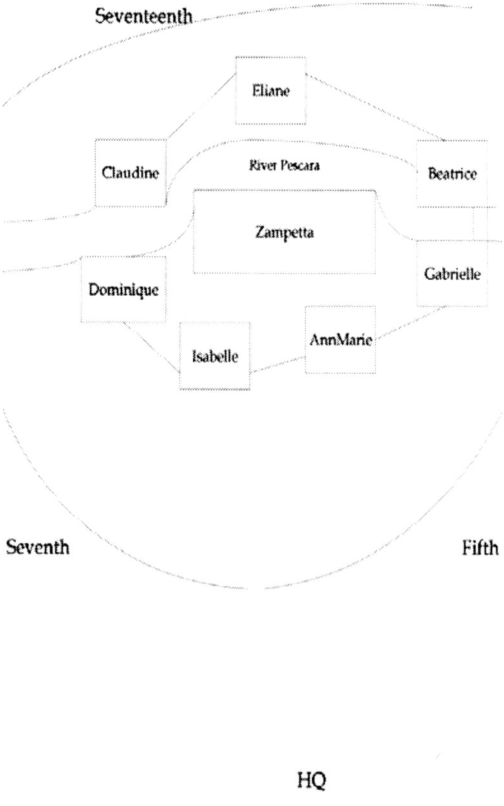

ABOUT THE AUTHOR

Born in 1956 in the East Anglian Fens in England he moved to Nottingham to study for his business degree. In line with the current myth of the time he met, courted and married a local girl and they have now been married for 30 years. They still live within 10 miles of Nottingham and have two adult children and have just become grandparents for the first time! Following a career in software development and IT management David was forced to give up work in 2005 to look after both his wife and daughter both of whom were suffering from different life threatening illnesses. To fill the time and take his mind off of the domestic and financial issues David eventually turned to his love of both photography and writing. Seven Sisters was the first product of the latter and has been followed by a prodigious number of works.

Lightning Source UK Ltd.
Milton Keynes UK
UKOW040625070313

207282UK00001B/12/P

9 781877 546259